Her anger was rising

"Mr. Powers," she said through clenched teeth. "This is a far better role than anything you've ever done before. This is the challenge of a lifetime. You've never been in a film that would require as much in-depth acting, as wide a variety of emotions as *Temptress* would allow."

"If I don't make your picture, Susan, who will?" His smile seemed more forced now, as though he were growing weary of this game between them. "Let's compromise. Give me a few funny scenes inside that sanitarium and a few more one-liners, and I'm all yours."

"I'm not interested in watering down this script, Mr. Powers."

"Then I'm not interested in doing this film, Susan." Without another word, Bruce Powers jumped up from the conference table and stalked out of the office.

Welcome to Hollywood, Susan, she thought. *You've finally made it, but you may not be staying long.*

Dear Reader,

Spellbinders! That's what we're striving for. The editors at Silhouette are determined to capture your imagination and win your heart with every single book we publish. Each month, six Special Editions are chosen with *you* in mind.

Our authors are our inspiration. Writers such as Nora Roberts, Tracy Sinclair, Kathleen Eagle, Carole Halston and Linda Howard—to name but a few—are masters at creating endearing characters and heartrending love stories. Their characters are everyday people—just like you and me—whose lives have been touched by love, whose dream and desire suddenly comes true!

So find a cozy, quiet place to read, and create your own special moment with a Silhouette Special Edition.

Sincerely,

Rosalind Noonan
Senior Editor
SILHOUETTE BOOKS

PAULA HAMILTON
Dream Lover

SILHOUETTE BOOKS

Copyright © 1990 by Paula Hamilton

All rights reserved. No part of this book may be used or reproduced in any manner whatsoever without written permission of the publisher.

Silhouette Special Edition

Published by Silhouette Books New York

America's Publisher of Contemporary Romance

SILHOUETTE BOOKS
300 East 42nd St., New York, N.Y. 10017

Copyright © 1986 by Paula Hamilton

ISBN: 0-373-09340-3

First Silhouette Books printing October 1986

SILHOUETTE, SILHOUETTE SPECIAL EDITION and colophon
are registered trademarks of the publisher.

America's Publisher of Contemporary Romance

Printed in the U.S.A.

PAULA HAMILTON

shares the basic characteristics of all writers—an insatiable curiosity and a deep love of books. She lives with her husband and two daughters on the edge of the Texas hill country, and when she isn't writing she may be found reading, golfing or trying to keep up with her busy family activities. She tries to begin each day with the intention of living life to the fullest and says the best way to do that is with lots of laughter.

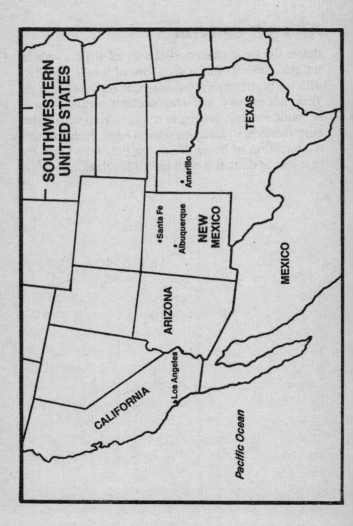

SOUTHWESTERN UNITED STATES

TEXAS

NEW MEXICO

• Santa Fe

• Albuquerque

• Amarillo

ARIZONA

CALIFORNIA

• Los Angeles

MEXICO

Pacific Ocean

Chapter One

Arriving at the airport with her airline ticket, two suitcases and a bag with her screenplay in it, Susan McCarthy tried not to be nervous. She had no idea what she was getting into. All she knew was that her agent, Larry Steinem, had sent a messenger with her ticket for the flight to Albuquerque, and a note saying he wished her all the best on her first location work for her movie, *Temptress*. The note also said that she shouldn't worry about carting her typewriter all the way to New Mexico; she'd have one available when she needed it. Now she was standing in the middle of the Los Angeles airport not knowing anything more than that.

She went up to the airline counter and was about to hand the agent her ticket. "Susan McCarthy. Paging Susan McCarthy." She heard her name being called by a nervous-looking young man who stood in the center of the walkway, dressed in a khaki uniform. She raised her hand. "Here," she said with a wave of her bag.

The man walked her way with hurried steps. "Miss McCarthy, I'm Joel Burton. I'm assigned to Mr. Powers for this movie and I've made a big mistake. I was supposed to arrange for you to fly in the private jet with Mr. Powers and a few others." His young face was etched with worry.

"I have my ticket. I'm leaving now," she told him, looking back at the commercial airliner outside the window.

"Yes, I know," he answered quickly. "But you see, Miss McCarthy, I made a mistake. I... Somehow your name wasn't on the roster that Mr. Powers sent me, and now he's waiting in the jet for me to bring you back."

"Oh, that's all right, really." Her anxiety was rising to meet that of this young man who was so obviously upset. "I can meet them in Albuquerque."

"No, ma'am." He looked panicked. "They're flying straight to Santa Fe." He went on. "Please, Miss McCarthy, come with me."

"It's that important that I come right now?" she asked, still not understanding the urgency.

He swallowed and his Adam's apple shot up and back down. He gave a short laugh that sounded more like a bleat. "It's very important. More than likely it means my job if I don't bring you with me."

She could see as well as feel his distress, and knowing what she did about Bruce Powers, the American Dream Lover, she knew this young man's feelings were more than likely well justified. Without anything more being said, she handed him her bags. "Let's go."

"Thanks, thanks a lot," he told her as he took her arm and began steering her in the opposite direction.

"What about this ticket?" she asked, thinking of how much a ticket from L.A. to Albuquerque must cost. In the brief time she'd been in Hollywood she still hadn't been able to adjust to the industry's blatant disregard for the cost of things.

"Don't worry. Give it to me. I'll take care of it." He was walking rapidly toward a ramp that was labeled with a sign for small planes. His grip on her arm hadn't loosened one bit.

Susan had wondered for the past three months what her reaction would be when she saw Bruce again. Now that it was coming sooner than she had expected, she felt a churning begin in the pit of her stomach. As much as she didn't want to see him, she realized she did. As much as she didn't want to be excited at the prospect, she was. Despite the arousal of emotion that the thought of being near him awakened, there was an accompanying cloud of gloominess. Bruce Powers was just another name for trouble.

Over and over again, she reminded herself how much a man like him could hurt a woman who might allow herself to care for him. She thought about it all the way to where his plane was waiting, kept thinking about it even when she stepped inside, even when she first saw Bruce sitting in the leather seat facing the only other empty one in the plane. His magnificent blue-black eyes were staring straight at her. His stare was hard, cold, unresponsive.

A flash of regret hit her, and she hesitated in the doorway. She stood there thinking she should have obeyed her first inclination and used her ticket for the commercial flight.

"Miss McCarthy," he said in that world-famous husky voice of his, "this is Mr. Fields—he's the associate producer for the picture—and Mr. Erskine, who has made the arrangements for our being accommodated so quickly while in Santa Fe. Gentlemen, I'd like you to meet Miss Susan McCarthy, our brilliant writer, who is going to be working closely with us throughout production."

His words sounded generous. The tone of his voice did not. It was a little like having a freezer door opened, hitting her with a full blast of cold air.

"Miss McCarthy, I apologize that our trip has not started off as smoothly as I had hoped," he said in formal tones. "Someone fouled up. You should have been told that you were to fly with us."

"That's all right," she said, brushing a hand through her hair before she sat down across from him.

"It won't happen again," he went on. "Remember, I intend to have you close to me throughout this movie."

Something intense was conveyed in his words—a warning, a threat? All she knew was that his unusual eyes were focused on her as if she were an unfamiliar specimen, and suddenly the idea of being close to him was more intimidating than she had ever dreamed.

When they were in the air, Bruce ignored her and began talking to the men about his expectations on arrival in Santa Fe. He discussed his role as both the star and director of the picture, and as Susan listened to him give orders with a smoothness brought on by experience, she was reminded of his absolute sovereignity in the industry.

Still, she had rejected him, the top box-office draw of 1984 and 1985, the Hollywood movie star voted America's choice as Mr. Dream Lover, the highest-paid star in the history of the industry. Not once but twice she'd rejected him.

It was probably the first time anything like that had ever happened to him. That would explain his indifferent behavior. If this was any indication of how things were to be between them, she could see right now that the road to her becoming an internationally acclaimed screenwriter as a result of working with him on this film was going to be a long and rocky one, indeed.

She fastened her seat belt, leaned back against the smooth leather seat and gave herself over to the tug of gravity that claimed the passengers of the Lear jet named *Dream Lover*. As they climbed, soaring up into the cloud bank, Susan closed her eyes to Bruce's disquieting stare and settled her head back, intent upon convincing him that she was asleep. But there was no sleep for her, not when she could feel his eyes boring into her, feel his overwhelming presence in the pressurized cabin.

Instead, she thought back over how much he had affected her life since the day a little over three months before when she had arrived in Hollywood and had taken out her carefully marked map so that she could find the sign on the side of the hill that said Hollywood. It was a long way from Texas to Tinseltown and a VIP suite in the Beverly Hills Hotel, particularly for a thirty-year-old woman who had never thought she'd spend more than six nights outside the city limits of dusty Amarillo. It seemed as if it had all happened ages ago, but she knew that it only felt that way because of how much her life had changed.

He'd been involved with every aspect of that change, this Dream Lover whose lips were soft and warm and whose arms had once held her so reverently.

Susan McCarthy was trembling with excitement, shaking with anticipation over this glorious day. With a deep breath she stepped out of the elevator and into the sprawling, opulent lobby of the Beverly Hills Hotel. She'd been in Los Angeles for a little less than sixteen hours and still she was dazed by all the moneyed splendor.

When Larry Steinem, her agent, waved and started toward her, she felt a shimmer of relief. All her life she'd dreamed of being here in the heart of filmdom and now that she'd made it, she was as nervous as a country mouse in the city. Back in Amarillo, her ultrasuede two-piece Levin suit of bright peacock blue and her simple gold jewelry would have gotten her plenty of compliments. Here, in this massive lobby full of the rich and famous, she couldn't help but feel a little overwhelmed.

"Hello, Susan. It's so good to see you. Welcome to California." Larry leaned over and planted a kiss on her forehead.

"Hi, Larry. I'm glad to be here... I guess."

They stood in the center of the lobby beneath a gleaming crystal chandelier. A colorful parade of people was scurrying around on all sides, but the two of them were staring hard at each other, smiles lighting both their faces. Susan was aware of a few passersby flicking guarded looks in her direction. She figured they were probably wondering who that unknown could be with Larry Steinem, one of Hollywood's most important agents.

"Hey, you're going to love it here. I promise."

Susan stepped back, curled her hands up to jam them into her suit pockets and then, thinking better of it, dropped her hands down to her sides. "I'm here. I'm staying," she said with a hint of firmness.

It was done. She'd left family, home and friends. She'd come thousands of miles to find fame and fortune in Hollywood. She'd planned the trip all her life. What she hadn't planned was being so full of anxiety.

"How did you sleep? Did you get a good night's sleep?"

Her blue eyes lit with amusement. "At these prices?"

Larry laughed. "Yeah."

"Are you kidding? The suite is as big as my apartment back in Amarillo. I practically took a bath in all the champagne they sent up. The bad part came when I woke up this morning in an immense bed in one of the most famous hotels in the world and I called down to ask for daily room rates." She batted her eyelashes. "Larry, when I asked you to make the arrangements for my stay you didn't understand. I wanted to spend a few nights here until I found more permanent digs. I didn't want to buy the place."

Laughing full out now, Larry took off his black-framed glasses and wiped the tracings of tears from the corners of his eyes. A short, gray-haired man with a bulldog face, Larry was earning his twenty-percent fee just by laughing at her halfhearted jokes. He made her feel far better.

"Come on," he said after he'd readjusted his glasses so that they gripped the short bridge of his nose. "On the way I'll give you my big-time lecture."

Larry made one small motion toward the uniformed man at the door, and as soon as he led Susan down the steps and out into the fresh California sunshine, his Mercedes was being delivered less than two feet from where they stood. Susan assumed this was a part of the Hollywood magic, too.

"You're going to have to put aside those old notions about frugality and conservation," Larry warned her. "You, my dear, are moving into the big time, and appearances can make or break a deal as quickly as anything else. Besides . . .'' He helped her into the car, but instead of shutting the door, he stood for a moment, looking down at her. "You, Miss McCarthy, are somebody now, and you are going to make me even richer than I already am."

Waiting for him to walk around to his side of the car, she took a moment to close her eyes. Relax and enjoy it, she told herself. You've paid your dues with hard work and faith in yourself.

But there were problems. Hollywood frightened her. It represented the epitome of self-indulgence, the dark side of success. She'd seen what it could do to people—suck them up and spit them out. Her best friend's brother had come to Hollywood and died here, a victim of too much too soon. She'd loosely based her script on his tragedy.

Once inside the car, Larry adjusted his thick glasses and headed toward downtown L.A. Susan watched him drive, and was again reminded of how glad she was that she had put herself in the capable hands of Larry Steinem. He was a man she could trust.

"Susan, I don't want you to be nervous, but I'm telling you that this is probably the most important meeting of your life. If your screenplay is made into a movie by Bruce Powers, you're going to be a hot property. You'll have it made." Larry carefully wove his way through the heavy L.A. traffic. "The man's more important than the national debt out here. He's money in everyone's pocket. Every director, every agent, every two-bit small-part actor wants to know him.''

She watched Larry's face light up as he explained more of the workings of Hollywood. She'd often fantasized about how Larry would look in his own environment. She'd met him face-to-face only twice before, and both times had been when he'd flown to Amarillo to talk to her. In the west Texas town of cowboys and pickup trucks, Larry had looked oddly out of place when he'd pulled up to her house in a chauffeured stretch limousine the size of a city block and stepped out dressed in black patent shoes with pointed toes and a suit so finely tailored that Susan wouldn't dare take a guess at its cost for fear she'd underrate the man's purchasing power. But here, in the land of cardboard sunshine and breezes from the ocean, he looked just right in his Mercedes 500 SL and his expensive suits. He looked like an agent for important people.

''Larry, the more you talk, the more I feel my heart doing drumrolls.'' She gave him a wide smile, feeling comfortable with the close relationship that had developed between the two of them in the weekly phone calls between Texas and California. ''You're telling me too much too fast. I can't absorb it all. What kind of agent are you, anyway?''

''The best kind,'' he answered with a roll of his head. ''The rich kind.''

She laughed then, grateful to have him beside her. If he'd assigned one of his assistants to go with her today, she'd have died. Still a little shaky about being in a strange place all alone, Susan wanted his support when she met the world-renowned producer, Evan Dirkson, the famous director Hal Mauldin and Bruce Powers.

"Tell me about this producer, Larry. Is he easy to talk to?"

"In a business known for being full of man-eating sharks, Evan Dirkson is a stellar example. He's a man with money and influence, and he uses both to get what he wants. Nobody messes with Evan."

Susan smoothed down the hem of her new blue suit with a nervous twist of her fingers and pulled down the sun visor, looking into the makeup mirror glued to its back. "Thanks. That's just what I needed." She took out a tube of lipstick and slashed the rose color across her lips. She stared briefly at her reflection. Back in the hotel suite she had wanted to do something different with her too-curly hair, but all she'd had time for was a little hair spray. Now she thought it looked too flat across the top and too wild around her ears. But it was too late to worry about her hair or anything else, for that matter, except how uneasy she was feeling.

Larry turned a corner, whisking the quiet-sounding Mercedes through a yellow light. "Hey, Susan, this is Larry. Have I ever lied to you?" He reached across the leather seats and put his hand out for hers. "I've made my money on my reputation. I don't lie to my clients or the people with whom I do business."

Susan patted his hand affectionately. "I know," she said with a nod. "I'm grateful, too."

"But Evan's not the one we have to worry about. There's only one man we have to convince in this meeting—Bruce Powers. If he says it's go, the rest of them, including all the studio heads, will be happy as bedbugs. Even Evan Dirkson doesn't have as much clout right now as Bruce Powers."

Susan squinted, looking out at the buildings they were passing. She reminded herself how it had been for the past few days when she'd been driving to L.A. Every now and then the smell of new leather had wafted through the closed-up Jag, and it was an aroma she had welcomed. To her it had smelled of fresh success. She didn't want to lose it, not when she was just beginning to find out how the real life of a screenwriter could be. Until very recently, it had meant days and nights spent at a typewriter, an aching back, no money and no recognition, save rejections.

"And don't forget the power of our own Miss Susan McCarthy," Larry was saying. He gave her an elaborate wink just as he pulled up to an ordinary-looking office building and parked the car.

"What's this?" Susan wondered.

"Evan's offices. He does all his business from here."

Susan looked at the brick-and-glass building. Across the front glass doors she saw Evan Dirkson's name etched. "I'm disappointed. I thought I was going to a studio. I thought I might see Al Pacino strolling down the studio sidewalks, or at least Walter Matthau."

"Sorry." Larry walked around and opened her door, noticing a spot on the door handle and taking a moment to wipe it away with a handkerchief. "But there'll be time enough for that soon. As soon as Powers says yes, you'll get to see your studio, my starstruck friend."

Nervously Susan took out her compact and looked at her reflection in the powder-caked mirror. "Am I really so obvious, Larry?" She saw the shine on the bridge of her nose and across her forehead between her brows, but there was no time for repair work. Larry was propelling her into the office building.

"Let's just call it a case of Hollywood fever. I'll arrange for you to have a tour of Mann's Chinese Theater where all the stars have their hand- and footprints in cement, and then I'll have someone drive you through Bel Air and points beyond for a tour of the stars' homes."

They were in the elevator riding up to the sixth floor. Larry had warned her how to deal with these people. He'd rehearsed her and rehearsed her, but she'd forgotten everything he'd said. Susan felt the weakness in her legs and the dryness of her throat. You're scared to death, she said to herself.

Larry had hold of her arm. "Remember, my dear, you told me you wanted to be a famous screenwriter more than you wanted anything else in the world. Convince Bruce Powers to take a chance on your script, and you've done it. Use that bright little mind of yours and above all, just be yourself."

"There's only one problem," she joked. "My self isn't accustomed to going to a meeting with world-famous people like these."

"Listen, Susan, and listen well," Larry said when they stepped out of the elevator. "I want to remind you of something." He pivoted her around so that she was facing him. "In Hollywood and points beyond, I'm known as a man who makes his clients famous. But the truth is that the only gift I have is a nose for talent. I can sniff out the best even if they're thousands of miles away. You've got it, my dear. Don't think for a moment that I would be wasting my time or my reputation with you if you didn't. Now let's go in there and show these men that Larry Steinem is right."

She managed a grateful smile. Larry was worth every percentage point he charged as her agent. "Okay," she whispered. "Okay."

The office they were led to by a silent secretary was so large that Susan thought it must consume the entire floor of the building. Paneled in dark oak and carpeted in dark purple, it was a little like a cave. There were heavy drapes across the back windows and the only lighting came from the lamps and gilt chandeliers. On three walls were immense oil paintings in the tradition of the old masters. Susan thought she recognized one of them as having been in an arts magazine she'd thumbed through a few months earlier, but surely it wasn't possible. The painting she'd read about was reputedly worth millions. She stared hard at it.

"Ah, Miss McCarthy, I see you admire fine art." From one side of the immense room a man stepped forward and started toward them. "I am Evan Dirkson." He put out his hand and she took it.

Dirkson was middle-aged. He wore a navy blue suit and a white shirt with a red-and-blue striped tie. He had a small goatee that from close up looked as if it were groomed as carefully as a woman's hair. It was thick and wavy, mostly gray, but each hair was cut so that the goateee came to a perfect point about two inches below his chin.

"I'm glad to know you, Mr. Dirkson." She was aware of being closely observed by the man but his expression was pleasant: he was probably as curious about her as she was about him. Larry had told her Dirkson had raved about her work. Larry had also claimed that the mere fact that Dirkson had made any positive comments about her at all should be cause for her to feel honored. Dirkson was powerful enough to have scripts coming to him every day—the very best scripts.

"May I introduce Hal Mauldin, Hollywood's finest director?" With a sweep of his hand, Dirkson half turned and Hal Mauldin stepped toward her.

"Pleased to meet you, Miss McCarthy." Hal Mauldin was older, a man of about sixty. He, too, had a face full of hair, but his was a full beard that looked as if it had never been brushed. He had a dark tan, a mouthful of yellowed tobacco-stained teeth and a wide grin. Dressed in wrinkled chino slacks, desert boots and a plaid shirt, Hal Mauldin looked as if he didn't fit in with the perfectly groomed Mr. Dirkson.

"Mr. Mauldin, I've long been an admirer of yours," she told him, not wanting to sound star struck, but unable to forget his fame as a top director.

"Larry." Evan shook hands with him and then motioned all of them over to a long conference table made of dark carved wood. "Bruce should be along any minute. I've taken the liberty of ordering coffee and tea for all of us. Shall we be seated?"

Susan took the offered chair between Larry and Hal Mauldin. Evan walked around the table and sat at the end. The chairs were enormous. Tapestry-covered, with ornately carved legs and arms, they were too big to be comfortable; Susan felt herself sink into the cushion until she was feeling small and intimidated. Maybe that's what it was all about, she thought, as she watched Evan pour coffee from a silver Georgian coffee service that looked to be antique. Maybe that was the way these Hollywood people did business. She looked over at Larry and he winked at her. Nothing intimidated him.

"I'm going up to Pebble Beach to play golf next Saturday, Evan. Want to come along?" Larry was asking.

"I might. Let me check my schedule later and I'll get back to you." He passed the eggshell-colored coffee cups and saucers to a man who served each of them, beginning with Susan, first handing out perfectly folded white embroidered napkins. When the man was finished, Evan dismissed him with a curt nod.

Larry was already sipping from his coffee cup. "I'd ask you, Hal, but I know you're not interested."

"Nope." Hal lit up a cigar, then, seeing the disdain on Evan's face, he put it out. "I'm going sailing."

As she sat there listening to the three of them talk among themselves, Susan felt herself pull back, thinking about the scene in front of her. Here she was, among three of the most important men in Hollywood, and they all thought she had something of value to offer them. It was a heady feeling. She could hardly believe it was true, but at the same time she reminded herself that she had to have talent or she wouldn't be there. Her self-doubts should be dismissed. These men, movers and shakers of the film industry, wanted her.

The door to the office swung open and Bruce Powers strode across the room, all six feet three inches of him. Suddenly, Susan felt the tension consuming her again as she turned to watch him approach.

"Sorry I'm late. Traffic's terrible out there. Besides, it's too early for a meeting, Evan. It's not even ten o'clock, for God's sake." Bruce Powers was complaining good-naturedly, a broad smile on his face.

Susan's immediate thought was that the man was almost beautiful, except for his blunt chin with the cleft. It was the only saving grace in a face that threatened to be too perfect. The cleft gave his face a hint of ruggedness.

She looked up into smoldering blue-black eyes that were half closed, the eyes that had made every woman who'd ever seen them on the screen think she was the one and only for Bruce Powers. It had been said by more than one interviewer that those smoky eyes of his made a woman believe he had some enormously satisfying secret that he was saving just for her. From this close proximity, Susan thought it was entirely true.

The movie cameras had captured his secret and displayed it on screens all around the world. He never took a bad picture. Those cameras don't do the man justice, she realized when he gave her one of his full smiles and started toward her.

"Miss McCarthy, this is a pleasant surprise," he said in that famous husky baritone of his. "I didn't expect anyone quite so attractive."

His eyes danced, laughing—at her, with her? She wasn't sure. She only knew he was a disturbing presence in an already stressful meeting.

Struggling to keep herself from blushing, Susan was silent, an openmouthed smile on her face.

"No one told me," he added with a dramatic shake of his head. "Or I would have made it a point to be here on time. I thought all I was going to see were these ugly mugs. I had no idea you'd be the bright light of this meeting."

Susan was struck with a sudden swell of disappointment. The feeling was as immense as anything she'd ever experienced. It wasn't that he wasn't saying the right things, but for all his charisma the man seemed to be operating on automatic. Where was the spontaneity? He sounded too much like some recorded message.

"You dogs," Bruce said, turning to the others. "You were trying to keep this all to yourselves, weren't you?" He took Susan's hand and held it in his own before giving her a broad wink intended to be flirtatious. His hand lingered on hers just a moment longer than she was comfortable with.

He's playing with me, she decided, feeling at once quite ill at ease. The famous Dream Lover who could knock a woman down from a distance of fifty yards was toying with her. He'd had so many women at his beck and call for so many years that he thought it was expected now. What a colossal disappointment.

As obtusely as she could, Susan withdrew her hand from his. She looked at Larry, who was watching her with guarded eyes, and she couldn't help wondering if her disappointment was obvious.

"Bruce, have a seat. Here, next to me." Evan Dirkson was the essence of politeness.

Watching the reactions of the others as they sought the star's attention, Susan reflected that when Bruce Powers had entered the room everything had changed. Was this what power and fame brought? Was it true that Hollywood affected people this way?

"I'll warn you early on about these two, Miss McCarthy." Bruce Powers was still talking to her as he went to sit where Evan Dirkson had pulled out a chair for him. "May I call you Susan?" He didn't wait for her to agree. "These men are thieves of the highest order. They'll ask you for your ideas and try to steal them for themselves. You mark my words."

He never took his eyes off hers as he talked. It made her uncomfortable, and she felt embarrassed by the entire situation. She'd expected too much of the man. He was as Hollywood as they came.

"But they'll come running back to buy your script because these two bums don't have your talent."

Everyone except Susan laughed. "And how do you know how much talent I have?" She gave him a direct look, her blue eyes unflinching.

It was Powers's turn to feel uneasy. He gave a half laugh. "I've seen the movie you wrote. *Stardust* was one of the finest Western romance films I've ever seen. If it had been a big-budget Hollywood film instead of an amateur regional production it would have received the recognition it deserved."

"Well, ladies and gentlemen, we're here to discuss making a movie together," Evan said. From the tabletop he picked up a bound copy of *Temptress*, Susan's new script.

Susan bent her head to retrieve her original copy of her manuscript, and as she did Bruce let himself look at her more fully than before. He thought her hair looked shinier than sunlight with flyaway curls the color of golden toast. She had an attractive face, not a movie-star face, but he found her very unusual. Sometimes the women who looked so right for the screen never looked as soft and appealing as some of those females who'd never performed before anything except a Polaroid One Step. He observed the slightly pointed chin and the delicate nose. She isn't even aware of it, he thought. She doesn't know how appealing she really is.

Bruce watched her turn the pages of the script. He noticed her perfectly tapered fingers and the gentle way she moved her hands. Yes, he told himself, you're right. She isn't aware of herself at all. If there was one thing Bruce Powers knew, it was women. He'd been around enough members of the opposite sex in his lifetime to classify and categorize all kinds. This one he would classify as unusual.

"I like this script, Susan. I really do." He took the copy Hal Mauldin handed him.

Bruce watched as she glanced momentarily at him, then moved her eyes instantly back to Evan Dirkson. Either she didn't understand that he was the one who'd decide whether they made this picture, or else she didn't like him. Bruce couldn't make up his mind which it was.

He tried again. "Of course everyone has his favorite scene, I'm sure, but I like the part where the hero goes into the sanatorium for cocaine abuse and is exposed to all kinds of crazies."

Evan Dirkson nodded in agreement. In less than two seconds, Susan saw Hal Mauldin's head beginning to move up and down. She wondered if anyone ever disagreed with Bruce Powers.

"You understand, don't you, that we'd allow... we'd want you to give us input as to who your co-star would be, Bruce?" Evan was stroking his beard as he spoke. "Somebody you'd be compatible with. Somebody you think you might like to work with on a daily basis.'' He gave Bruce a conspiratorial grin. ''Linda Lansing might be good for the role.''

From the pages of *Variety*, Susan was aware that Bruce's current love interest was Linda Lansing, a platinum blonde with breasts that would make the common man swoon, and the acting talent of an ant. Susan wrinkled her nose but said nothing.

Hal Mauldin spoke up. ''Linda's never done a part this heavy. She's more suited for sitcoms.'' He looked at Bruce, whose eyes were turned toward Susan, then he looked at Evan. ''But if you think she can do the job, we can discuss it.'' When he got no response, he started backtracking. ''Who knows, she might be perfect for the part.''

''Let's talk about that later, Hal. I'm interested in hearing from Susan. I want to know how she sees this film project. What do you think, Susan? How do you see this project unfolding on the screen?''

Susan studied the handsome face before her, the perfect aristocratic nose, the wide blue-black eyes surrounded by thick lashes and covered with a strong curve of brow. He was unbelievably attractive, but he was a little too smooth, too polished for her. She'd dreamed of meeting him for so long and now she was almost sorry she had. The illusion was tarnished like an unused brass pot.

''I see it just as it's written,'' she answered him, after taking a few seconds to decide precisely what she'd say. Her voice was low but steady.

Bruce put both elbows on the table and leaned across it, looking only at her. ''But, Susan, do you see any humor being added? I'm wondering if it isn't just a little too stiff in places."

He'd made most of his money in movies that emphasized zingy one-liners and car chases. Over the years his comedic talent had improved until now he was thought of as not only a handsome star but a major comedian. Susan wondered how much that had to do with his question. Then she wondered whether he really misunderstood the project enough to see it as lending itself to humor.

"Do you see this as a humorous movie?" Evan asked Bruce before Susan could reply.

"Well—let's just say I think there's room for a little lightness."

"I hadn't thought of it that way, but give me your ideas," Evan continued, oblivious to everyone else at the table except Bruce Powers.

"I was hoping Susan would talk to us about the movie idea and then we could all interact here together." Bruce gave Susan one of his most winning smiles, lips fully open, toothy, rich. It was the one he'd perfected for *Ghostrunner* when he'd gotten his first big break. Now it was a part of him, but back then he'd had to practice it in the mirror until he thought his mouth might crack from the strain.

Taking her time to think of an appropriate answer, Susan took a deep breath, trying to steady her nerves and calm her racing heart. When she spoke, it was in a solemn voice.

"I wrote this as a story of a man who has everything in the world going for him, a beautiful wife, a thriving career, and two loving children. Then one night he's offered a little cocaine at a party, and just for fun he tries it. Over the next few months he begins using it more and more. It's a social drug, a quick high, he explains to his wife, and then he gets her involved with coke, too. But something happens to this man and suddenly the cocaine is in control of him. It's got him and it won't let go. I intended that this be a powerful story of one man's struggle through hell to survive."

When she finished, no one spoke. Then Bruce said, "Yes, but I still think there should be some funny lines in this script."

"I had thought there were a few, especially in the first part of the script, but I'll be happy to go back and sharpen them up if you like." Susan felt good after describing her story, a tribute to her friend. To her ears, it had sounded solid and strong. The reactions from the others at the table had been good, too. She could feel it.

"That's fair enough," Hal Mauldin interjected, looking to Bruce for agreement.

Leaning back in his chair, Bruce Powers was frowning. "I don't know." He looked directly at Evan Dirkson. "I see this as something more like *One Flew Over the Cuckoo's Nest*, an Academy Award winner."

Evan Dirkson listened, then began drumming his fingers on the tabletop. "That would call for a major rewrite, Bruce. As it stands now, the story can't be compared to that film. It's too serious—more like *The Lost Weekend* with Ray Milland."

"I don't think my fans want to see me as Ray Milland. They like me funny." Abruptly, Bruce pushed himself forward until his elbows were on the conference table holding up his chin. His face was set, firm.

"That sounds good to me," Hal interrupted again.

"Yes, well, I have no objections. We'll make money with Bruce Powers. We know that," Evan replied.

"Good," Bruce said, and his expression had softened and his happy-go-lucky look returned.

"Now, wait a minute." Susan fought to keep her voice from rising. Larry had warned her of this very thing, but hearing about it from him was quite different from seeing her work bandied about as though it had no value.

"Yes?" Evan's expression was one of tolerance, as if it was expected that every beginning screenwriter would say exactly those words at exactly this time.

"I don't argue with the comparison of *Temptress* as being like *One Flew Over the Cuckoo's Nest*. You, Mr. Dirkson...I think you had it pictured much more correctly with your comparison to *The Lost Weekend*. This is a dramatic story of what drug abuse can do. It's a serious story of how a man can prove himself to be even stronger than he thinks he's capable of being. I see it as humorous, touching, revealing, but not with the same degree of humor as in *Cuckoo's Nest*."

His frown returning, Bruce turned to look at her, letting his arms fall to the table. He shrugged his shoulders. "I just don't see it that way. Furthermore, my fans wouldn't see it that way."

Her anger was rising. Her face felt flushed. "Mr. Powers," she said through clenched teeth, "this is a far better role than anything you've ever done before. This is the challenge of a lifetime. You've never been in a film that would require as much in-depth acting, as wide a variety of emotions as *Temptress* would allow."

She could sense the tension in the room among the others, who by now had become casual observers of a play being acted out by only two participants—one a too-slick movie star, the other a not-too-well-known screenwriter. As furious as she was, she had the sinking feeling that she was waging a battle with a force far too strong for her. If Bruce Powers didn't make her movie, Evan Dirkson and Hal Mauldin wouldn't want to make it, either.

"I'm sure, Susan, that every screenwriter believes their script is perfection at its best. I just think it's a little too serious. It needs a little comedy, a little fun." He grinned at her as if he was so accustomed to getting his way that he'd tolerate her ignorance just a little while longer. "As for my acting ability, I'm sure you've heard the story that I got fired about ten years ago from Columbia Pictures." He issued a mocking laugh. "Columbia Pictures would do anything to get me back now. Ask the chairman of the board."

"I don't doubt that you're right," she acknowledged.

"If I don't make your picture, Susan, who will?" His smile seemed more forced now, as though he were growing weary of this game between them. "Let's compromise. Give me a few funny scenes inside that sanatorium and a few more one-liners and I'm all yours." He spread his hands apart when he spoke his final words.

"I'm not interested in watering down this script, Mr. Powers." She felt Larry's hand touch her knee under the table in silent warning.

"Then I'm not interested in doing this film, Susan." His words were a scalding denunciation of the nervy woman sitting across from him.

"Miss McCarthy, you must reconsider if you want to see your script made into a film," Evan Dirkson warned her.

She looked at the troubled expression on Larry's face and the surprised looks of the producer and director. She knew what they were thinking: how dared she throw away a career like this.

"Go ahead," she snapped. "Screw the script up until you get the sort of mushy pabulum you like so well. Go on and write it the way you see it." She slid her manuscript across the table and watched him catch it before it landed in his lap. "Because if you don't respect your abilities any more than that, I certainly won't waste my time with it, either."

Without another word Bruce Powers jumped up from the conference table and stalked out of the office, throwing her script to the floor as he left the room.

She watched him go, in shock at the way she'd let him have it with both barrels, sure that she'd ruined her chances for fame and fortune. Well, she thought, she certainly hadn't taken the risk of selling herself out. No chance.

Welcome to Hollywood, Susan, she thought. *You've finally made it, but you may not be staying long.*

Chapter Two

Stark silence filled the room like creeping wet cement. Susan kept her head down, knowing she was being stared at by more than one pair of eyes.

Evan Dirkson cleared his throat. "Ahemm..."

She knew he was waiting for her to look at him. Finally she did so and was rewarded with a look from him full of all the anger she'd anticipated.

"You told Mr. Powers that he didn't think much of his own talents." Dirkson ran his bony fingers through his goatee.

She waited, aware of the leaden anger in his voice. The waiting was like knowing you were about to be pounced on but not knowing which way to move for escape.

Dirkson jerked his chair back and stood up, the force of his words matching the force of his movements. "Well, let me tell you, little lady from nowhere, you've just shown me how little you think of your own. You're new to Hollywood. You've got a lot to learn, and now that you've pulled this stunt you may not have long to learn it."

He turned his anger on Larry. "If we lose Bruce Powers over this little...little Miss What's-her-name, then you'd better put her back on the next bus to Texas." He walked over and stood behind Susan for a second, then leaned down over her shoulder. "Because I'll see that she doesn't sell anybody a script in this town—ever."

"Her point was well made, Evan. Nobody in this room can deny that. Her script reads right just as it is." Larry stood up and faced the producer, maintaining a calm voice and conciliatory stance.

"But," Dirkson hissed, "it doesn't make a hell of a lot of difference, because without Powers none of us has a picture."

"He'll be back," Larry insisted with a sureness that surprised Susan in its absoluteness. "Wait and see." He pulled Susan's chair back for her and they started out of the room.

"She's the one who'd better worry about waiting to see. Not me."

As Larry whisked her out of the office and down the elevator, Susan blocked out what she'd done. She kept thinking of how Dirkson had tried to act as if she were the only one worrying, but his eyes hadn't lied. He was afraid.

Larry guided the Mercedes back down the same streets they'd traveled earlier in the day. Only this time the atmosphere was different. Larry was silent, his jawline firm and pronounced as if he were tightening up all the muscles around his mouth at once. His head remained still, his eyes focusing straight ahead.

Susan felt as uneasy as she'd ever remembered. The silence between them was heavy, oppressive. She felt as though she'd betrayed her best friend.

After they'd traveled for a good fifteen minutes, she said, "Aren't you going to say anything?"

"I'm thinking."

"Oh."

"You were very effective back there."

"I guess I really fouled things up, huh?"

"Fouled things up? I don't think so. I'm not worried about it, anyway."

He gave her a quick analytic glance. He understood what she must be feeling.

"You're not?" she ventured. "I don't know why not. I probably just cost you a commission."

"The script will sell. It may now become a question of where, but I still think Powers is interested. You really got to him with your comment, I think."

Remorse engulfed her. This wasn't happening as she'd planned. She'd thought she'd go into a meeting with all those men and come out happier than she'd ever been in her life, knowing that fame and fortune were waiting for her at the end of the picture. *Temptress* could be an Academy Award winner; she'd believed that since its inception.

"I shouldn't have thrown that script at him."

Larry shrugged. "You took a calculated risk. Maybe it will make him think."

Susan pondered the problem. She was a newcomer to the world of moviemaking but she knew enough to know that a screenwriter was about as important as the assistant to the assistant to the assistant director. Once a screenplay was bought, it became public property and everyone and anyone could take a shot at it. She'd heard all the stories of how many screenplays never made it to the screen as the writer had intended because the producer, the director, the actors and even the support crew offered ideas and lines that could be thrown into a script.

Why had she done this? Because she wanted to show these people that she wouldn't sacrifice her principles? If so, she'd made a big mistake in judgment. These people didn't give a damn about her principles. They wanted to make a movie that would make them money and bring them recognition. Her script was just a vehicle, a way of getting there—one way. There were many others.

"I may have gone too far."

Larry was pulling up to her hotel. "Don't worry about it." He stopped the car and the doorman came to open Susan's door, but Larry waved him away. "Remember what he said. The script's good. You're good. I'm not saying Powers will end up doing it, but it will sell to someone down the line."

The doorman stood with one hand on the door handle, waiting for her. "What should I do, Larry?" she asked.

"Wait. That's all we can do. If I get a call, you'll hear from me right away. Don't go too far from the phone."

"Larry, I..."

"Hey," he said softly. "You've had your first introduction to Hollywood meetings. Don't start worrying until I tell you. Dirkson may call us back."

"It's not like me to react so strongly," she said, feeling a sharp pang of helplessness.

"You reacted that way because you believe in it. That's why. And one thing about it, those guys will certainly remember your name." He leaned across the seat and kissed her cheek. "I'll send someone by this afternoon to give you a tour of Hollywood. Be out here at two o'clock on the nose."

She started to get out and then she heard him laughing. "I'll never forget the look on Bruce Powers's face. You had him crazy there for a minute."

"Larry..."

"I'll be talking to you, kid." He readjusted himself behind the wheel and put the car into drive. "I'll be talking to you."

She watched Larry drive away and her thoughts turned back to Bruce Powers. Never in her thirty years could Susan recall having seen anything quite so fascinating as the sight of Bruce Powers sitting across

from her at that immense table. He was a real Dream
Lover. Even when he'd stalked out of the room, he'd
done it impressively.

A lump rose in her throat. No wonder this place
drove people to distraction. She felt as if she'd jumped
on a runaway car. Her control over her own destiny
was being threatened, and she felt almost as though
she were in a Hollywood film. She was being threatened by the most handsome leading man she'd ever
seen.

When the Rolls-Royce pulled up in the circular
driveway, Bruce jumped out before the driver had
brought the car to a full stop. He stormed through the
front doors of his Beverly Hills mansion, still seeth-
ing with anger.

*Let some beginner of a screenplay writer get under
your skin and march out like a damned fool,* he
thought with disgust. *Someday it's going to catch up
with you, this temper of yours, Bruce, my friend.* The
woman had touched some raw nerve and brought it to
life with unexpected pain. He'd gone crazy with emotion.

He threw open the doors of his library and strode
purposefully across the Oriental rugs and highly polished teakwood floor over to the coffee table, picked
up a cigarette from a Baccarat crystal holder and lit it
with a matching lighter. One puff made him cough.
After two he snapped the filter off between his thumb
and finger, then inhaled hard.

"Boss, I put the car— Boss, I thought you weren't going to smoke anymore." Johnny Day, his body-guard and driver, had walked in behind him. He stood in the open doorway, all six feet six of working muscle. He looked perplexed.

"I'm not."

"Yeah, but you're smoking," Johnny said in his gruff boxer's goice.

"Brilliant, Johnny. Now get out of here and close the doors behind you." The look in Bruce Powers's eyes said he meant business.

Hurriedly Johnny did as he was told, taking care to close the library doors with ease.

After he was sure the door was securely shut, Bruce ground the cigarette out in the brass ashtray. Then he took the cigarettes that were left in the crystal holder and carelessly tossed them into the marble fireplace, unmindful of the mess. The maid would take care of them as soon as he left the room.

He went to stand at the French doors that looked out on his property. Through the panes of glass, he was able to see one edge of the tennis courts and most of the long rectangular pool he'd had designed for swimming laps. Usually when he stood here survey-ing all that he had been able to attain, he felt a surge of well-being run through him. It brought about a sense of accomplishment and in turn it made him feel better, no matter what the problem.

Why did you behave that way, he complained to himself. Why let that woman upset you? What differ-ence could her opinion possibly make?

Unconsciously, he tugged at his ear, a gesture of his father's he'd copied from a time long past. Is it because you're thinking the same thing she's thinking? That you're afraid to take on a part that would require you to dig down into yourself as an actor? He repeated the same muddling thought over and over again in his mind until the words ran together in one blur.

"Johnny," he yelled out. "Come in here." He could hear the man's footsteps echo down the marble-tiled hallway. Bruce was never far away from people now that he'd become famous. All he had to do was call and someone came running. At first it had been important to him. Now it seemed a growing nuisance. He wished there was some way he could be alone, all alone.

"Yes, sir." Johnny opened one of the doors and peered into the room, a wide smile on his face.

"Let's go to Las Vegas, spend the night, gamble a little, have some fun." Bruce forced himself to smile. There was no reason for him to be moody, he warned himself. He'd have to snap out of it.

"Sure enough, boss. I'll call for the plane." Johnny stepped into the room and walked to the French cradle phone on the antique Honduran walnut desk. He picked up the receiver and turned to glance at his boss. "I sure am glad you're in a better mood."

Bruce was a thousand miles away, his eyes staring down at the fireplace where the cigarettes lay strewn about. "I guess I've been in a foul mood a lot lately, haven't I?" he said in a distant voice.

"I didn't want to say anything, but yeah, you have. Course it's hard on a man trying to give up cigarettes and all." Johnny tried to excuse him.

But I know the real truth, Bruce thought to himself. I'm a forty-year-old movie star who's made a fortune out of movies where I grin into the camera and hop into a fast car and drive the pretty girl around the block. I'm a movie star, all right, but am I ever going to be an actor? That's what he'd come to Hollywood for twelve years before. He'd come to be the best actor of his time. He'd come to win an Academy Award.

But the public had liked him as a star. The one time he'd tried to do a serious film, it had been a box-office failure—a bomb that still made him cringe with remorse. Could he be an actor, Bruce wondered. It was something that had been bothering him more and more lately. Susan McCarthy had given him one look today and had had her doubts. He'd sensed her skepticism. Strangely enough, he felt the same way.

"Hey, boss, should I call Miss Lansing? See if maybe she wants to go with us? Your secretary said she'd been calling."

Bruce thought of Linda Lansing. Then he thought of Susan McCarthy. The two women weren't anything alike. "Yeah, call Linda. Tell her to be ready in thirty minutes." Linda knew how to make a man relax—in bed at least. Susan McCarthy wouldn't hold a candle to Linda Lansing. Not one single candle. "Tell Linda I said to make it fifteen. I'm ready to get out of town."

* * *

At two o'clock Susan was dressed and standing outside the Beverly Hills Hotel. She looked forward to seeing the sights. She'd wanted this for a long time, but now she wished she wasn't going. The excitement had been drained from her after the morning's fiasco, drained until there was nothing left. She was tired. Tired and disappointed.

"Hi, Susan." A middle-aged woman with sleek brown hair and a smiling face pulled up in front of her in a red El Dorado convertible. "I'm Louise Tate. Hop in."

"You're Louise?" Susan exclaimed as she hurriedly got in beside the attractive woman.

"None other." Louise Tate stuck out her hand and when Susan took it, she gave her a quick handshake, her smile growing. "I'm here to take you on your tour."

"I'm so glad it's you," Susan said as they drove away, the wind blowing through her curly blond hair. Susan had spoken to Louise many times on the telephone. She felt as if they knew one another pretty well.

"I have a special in with the boss. You're just what I imagined, studying everything you see as if it were going in to your next screenplay."

Louise put on a pair of tortoiseshell sunglasses, covering up her dark eyes, which were made up a little like Elizabeth Taylor's in *Cleopatra*. Susan watched, thinking of how much younger Louise was than she'd expected. Dressed in a khaki linen dress with billowing sleeves, concealed buttons and an un-complicated neckline, Louise was an extremely at-tractive, impressive-looking woman. The longer Susan looked at her, the more she appreciated the simple style, the casual yet confident bearing of the woman.

"That's a lovely dress," Susan told her.

"Calvin Klein, off the rack."

"Oh."

"I'll take you shopping soon, if you like." Louise glanced over at Susan's plain blue wool skirt and white cotton sweater.

Susan started laughing. "I don't look like I belong here, do I?"

"You're fine," Louise protested.

"I'm fine, but I'm hot. Back in Amarillo, we're still having cold blue northers. Besides I've been watching all the women who come into the hotel. Is it Califor-nia tradition or my imagination that the women around here are either so overdressed they look like they belong in Paris or so casual they could cook hot dogs in the hotel lobby?"

At that, Louise really began to laugh. She adjusted her glasses and looked at her passenger, unable to control herself. "How perfect," she cried out. "Ut-terly perfect. No wonder you're on your way to being a famous screenwriter. No one could have said it bet-ter."

Susan leaned back in the soft leather seat and crossed her arms. "I wouldn't be so sure about that," she said sadly. "And I don't think you'll have to worry about taking me shopping. I may be out of Los Angeles before I have a chance to go anywhere within the city limits.''

Louise steered the smooth-riding car up onto a freeway, and suddenly they were immersed in a sea of bumper-to-bumper traffic. ''Larry told me to take you to see where the stars put their handprints—the Chinese Theater. When we get there, I don't want you to be disappointed. The place is definitely not what it used to be.''

''I won't.''

Louise considered the glum expression on Susan's face. ''Hey, don't let it get you down. You've just gotten here. It's a crazy place to be, but you'll get used to it.''

Susan gave her head a vehement shake. ''Hardly. After today I feel like I've been chewed up and spit out by a garbage truck.''

The traffic kept them traveling at a snail's pace. Louise tilted up her rearview mirror and turned off the radio that she always kept going except when she was about to have a serious conversation. Her wide brown eyes took on an earnest expression.

''Hey,'' she said. ''Larry told me about it.'' She caught the surprise in Susan's face. ''In case you didn't already know it, my dear, Larry and I are . . . friends. Close friends. He tells me everything.''

A new appreciation came over Susan as she looked at Louise. No wonder she was so confident. She had everything: a glamorous job and the boss.

''Then you know what I've done.''

''Indeed I do,'' Louise answered.

"I'll bet no one has crossed Bruce Powers since the first day he came to Hollywood, and I go and do it less than an hour after we meet."

Louise nodded her understanding, and that was all the encouragement Susan needed to continue. She needed someone to talk to, and right now Louise was the only person in Los Angeles who'd listen.

"Larry had already warned me about how a screenplay is treated. He'd told me that once I sold it I'd lose control of it, but I couldn't believe my ears when I heard that...that movie star talking about twisting my beautiful script into some comedic vehicle for his own ego. It's too good for that, Louise." Susan's lower lip was quivering with emotion, and she told herself she was way past the point of being tired. She was exhausted; otherwise, she wouldn't be displaying her insecurities on so grand a scale.

Louise reached over and patted her arm. "I know how you feel, kid. I know."

Susan wiped her hands across her face, then looked out across the lanes of traffic. "I probably should have kept my cool."

"That depends."

"On what?"

"On whether you believe in it that strongly or not. Larry and I have discussed *Temptress* and we think it's got award potential. I can understand your not wanting it to be any less than what it was when you wrote it."

"You can?" Susan asked with mild surprise. "Really?"

"Really, and so can Larry. He's still laughing over Powers's expression." Louise nodded, then turned silent as she spotted a hole in the traffic in front of her and gave all her attention to steering the Cadillac into the vacant spot. She flipped on the blinker as they neared the exit ramp.

"Then what would you do if you were in my place? I mean, I don't want to be sent packing back to Amarillo, without selling a script, but anybody can write Bruce Powers another silly movie."

They eased off the expressway and Louise put her foot on the brake, stopping at a red light. "Are you asking for advice?" Louise waited until Susan said yes before plunging in with her opinions.

"Then I'll tell you what I think. I think you're going to have to decide whether you want to write scripts and hold on to them until they're done as you want them done, or whether you want to join the ranks of writers who turn out what a star and a director want. They are not one and the same, believe me. The only thing I can tell you is that I've seen it happen time and time again. I can introduce you to other writers, but they'll tell you the same thing. You can keep your principles, but you may not sell for a long time, or you can wait until the day comes when you find a producer and a director—and a star—who are all willing to accept your material as it is. That's the long and the short of it."

Over and over again, Susan's mind combed over Louise's words. Through the long afternoon, as Louise drove her from place to place, to Mann's

Chinese Theater, to Westwood, to the studios of Universal and Columbia, Susan kept her eyes on the sights before her, and her mind on what her new friend had said. Susan made up her mind that if another meeting were called, she would leave herself open for some compromises but not so many that her script would be destroyed.

After declining Louise's offer to have dinner with her, Susan went back to her hotel room and ordered from room service. While she waited for her order to be delivered, she took a hot shower, trying to wash away the exhaustion along with the day's grime.

She threw one of the complimentary white terry robes around her and hurriedly tied its sash as she went to answer the knock at the door. The food looked good—marinated breast of chicken over wild rice and a glass of white wine—but she made the mistake of sitting on the edge of her bed to eat. Before she'd finished the third bite, her eyes began to close, and Susan gave herself up to the way she was feeling. She eased herself down across the bed and closed her eyes, pulling up the edge of the bedspread to wrap around her, not even bothering to put the pillow under her head, but using her arm instead. She was too tired to care.

The next morning she was awakened by the clamorous ring of the telephone beside her bed. With her heart skipping madly, she grabbed the phone. As sleepy as she was, the thought of whom it might be brought her instantly awake.

"Yes," she said breathlessly.

"Susan, it's Larry."

She couldn't tell from the sound of his voice whether it would be good news or bad. She tried to prepare herself for the worst.

"Hello, Larry."

"You've got one more shot, my dear. Mr. Powers himself has called from Las Vegas. He wants us to attend a meeting at four o'clock this afternoon."

"Oh, God!" she exclaimed.

"Susan, I want to talk to you before the meeting. Let's say we'll meet for lunch in the Polo Lounge at one-thirty."

"Yes," she cried. "That will be fine."

"And, Susan," he said softly. "You know what I want to talk about. Between now and this afternoon, you're going to have some decisions to make."

"I know, Larry. I know."

"We'll talk about what you're going to do in the meeting."

"All right," she replied and wiped her hand across her face.

"Powers is bound to have given your comments some thought," he said before telling her goodbye.

Long after the call was finished, she held the receiver in her hand. So much was riding on what went on between Bruce and herself. So much.

Chapter Three

Mr. Lazar, Mr. Diamond, please call the hotel operator." The pleasantly soft voice announced the famous names as though they belonged to ordinary citizens.

"I've never been in the same room with so many famous people," Susan said to Larry after they'd ordered hot chicken salad.

The Polo Lounge was crowded, darkly lit, but not so dark that she couldn't recognize faces she'd seen on the screen. The service was slow, but Susan didn't mind. It gave her more opportunity to take in everything she was seeing.

"You'd be surprised at how many Hollywood deals are made here, Susan." Larry hesitated and then spoke in a whisper. "Don't turn around, but Warren Beatty is standing behind you."

"Hey, Larry. Good to see you." Warren Beatty passed by their table, tapping Larry's shoulder before walking out of the Polo Lounge.

"I shouldn't have brought you here," Larry told her when he saw the look of astonishment on her face. "You won't be able to concentrate." He laughed. "Everyone comes to Hollywood thinking it's Mecca."

"Go ahead, make fun, but another day or two and I'll be as blasé as you Hollywoodites." She took her eyes off the broad shoulders of the star leaving the room and gave Larry her full attention. She smiled softly. "Besides, I've already made up my mind about what I'm going to do, and you can see for yourself that I'm quite content."

Larry stared at her for a second; she did have a self-satisfied look about her. She wasn't nearly as tense as she'd been the day before. He wondered if he'd misjudged this bright young woman sitting across from him. If he had, it would be one of his rare mistakes. "So how about filling me in as to how you've found contentment? I may want to use your approach."

"I've thought it over, Larry, and I intend to go into that meeting today ready for however those people behave. But it's still my script, and I won't let them turn it into Howdy Doody's show of shows."

He watched her closely, wondering if he could predict how deep her determination went. This could be a rough day for her. It was the first time she'd had her script subjected to restructuring, and yesterday she hadn't taken it at all well. If Larry's instincts about the woman had been correct, she'd come out okay. After yesterday, Louise certainly believed in her.

"I had a long talk with Louise, and this morning she had a book delivered to my room. It was written by Peter Franks, telling all about his life as a scriptwriter."

She'd studied the book, combing through each paragraph as she'd sought a way to identify with the author. Reading a peer's factual accounting of how the business really operated had been quite a revelation.

"And?"

"And he says it's hell, but that's show business. Your work is never your own once it's sold."

"Peter Franks is one of the most talented men in this town, but what you read shouldn't be news to you. I already explained it all."

"Yeah, but I needed the reinforcement." She'd been gesturing as she spoke, but put her hands down in her lap when the waiter delivered the chicken salad.

"And now?"

"Now," she said, taking a bite, "I'm going to hold on to what I've got. I want a commitment that this won't be turned into just another Bruce Powers vehicle for comedy. I'm willing to make some concessions, but I won't have this script ruined."

Larry shook his head. "You're really something, you know it? Spirit, that's what you've got. The first time she spoke to you on the telephone, Louise said you had it. After your little trip yesterday, the woman's more convinced than ever. She likes you."

"That's good to hear," she said, "but as for the spirit, we'll soon see. All the things you warned me about are becoming reality. This isn't an easy place to be." She reached out and put her hand over his as he was lowering his fork to his plate.

He shrugged his shoulders, then tilted his head toward her in a conspiratorial fashion. "Nothing like this is every easy. Working with people like these is never easy, and the fact that we're dealing with something very big here doesn't help."

She nodded, watching his bulldog face wrinkle up as he spoke. She was telling herself that she had learned the hard way what the consequences might be. Now she'd have to always keep in mind what Franks had said in his book. "In L.A. more than anyplace else in the world, the life of a screenwriter is a cutthroat, competitive business, and the ones who survive may not be the most talented. They may have known when the time was right to keep their mouths shut. They may have had the luck of the angels visited upon them."

Finishing their lunch, the two of them talked of other things. Deeply interested in learning everything she could about the movie business, Susan drowned Larry with questions. Infinitely patient, Larry answered each question with care and then told her anecdotes about Hollywood life that left her alternately speechless or laughing.

At three-fifteen, Larry said, "Knowing L.A. traffic, I suggest we get ourselves over to Dirkson's office. We wouldn't want to be late."

"No. We wouldn't want that at all." Susan followed him out of the Polo Lounge, aware of the many eyes glancing in their direction. She wondered how people got used to being watched. Larry didn't seem to notice.

She was calm all the way to Dirkson's office. She felt she'd made her decision and she could be comfortable with it. But once they stepped inside the elevator, she felt her insides begin to squirm. She curled her fingers into a fist and felt her nails dig into her palm. She had to get used to these tedious, tense meetings if she wanted to succeed, but she wondered if they ever got easier.

When they were led into Dirkson's office, they were told he wasn't there but would be in a few minutes. They waited in silence, the doubtful part of Susan taunting her as the moments ticked by. She made herself stare at the paintings she'd admired yesterday.

When Hal Mauldin walked in and shook hands with both of them, she began to feel better once again, and by the time Evan Dirkson entered the office she had shaken off the plaguing anxiety.

"I'm sorry I was late. I had rushes to see of our latest comedy adventure." Today Dirkson was wearing an expensive navy pin-striped suit. His goatee was perfectly groomed, his expression serious.

Susan watched Hal Mauldin crush out the cigar he'd lit only seconds earlier. The mood in the room was different from the day before. Mauldin was more nervous than ever, Dirkson was decidedly cool and Powers was late again.

"How do the rushes look?" Larry asked.

Evan gave Larry a quick glance. "Good," he said with what Susan thought might be false enthusiasm. She wondered if any of these people ever said what they really believed about a picture to anyone else.

"Before Mr. Powers arrives, I want to say that I assume we're all in agreement here. We're interested in making a picture. We're going to work to make certain that Mr. Powers likes it. Is that agreed?" Evan looked first at Susan, his beady eyes hard with intent.

Larry chose to answer him. "We need to agree first on the script, Evan."

"I'm looking for assurance that there will be no more outbursts like those yesterday," Dirkson said nastily.

"You have my assurance." Susan looked directly at him.

"I'm glad to hear that," Dirkson said as he ran his fingers across his goatee. Then he looked down at his gold watch.

The door opened and Bruce Powers entered. He was dressed in a long-sleeved white cashmere vee neck sweater with navy slacks and navy Gucci loafers. The white sweater contrasted with his tanned bronze skin, bringing out the stark blackness of his hair. He wore a thick gold chain around his wrist and a gold coil ring on his left hand. Susan noticed that his fingernails were perfectly manicured, buffed to a soft roundness. Everything about the man said "star."

"I can't believe you all beat me here again," he said with a disarming grin. "I apologize." He looked around at the others before letting his eyes come to rest on Susan. His smile grew, then mellowed.

"That's all right," Larry told him. "We haven't been here long, at all."

After a round of handshakes, Evan Dirkson showed them to the conference table. Each of them sat in exactly the same place as the morning before. Susan was aware that Bruce Powers had not shaken hands with her. She'd stood there waiting, expecting it, but he'd passed her by.

"Okay," Bruce said, taking over the meeting immediately. "I've thought about this script, and I've decided I want to do it."

For a moment no one spoke. Hal Mauldin looked cautiously over at Susan. The room was tense.

"Good." Dirkson spoke up. He smiled. "What suggestions do you have?"

Bruce glanced first at Susan, then at the producer. "Do you want specifics?"

"Of course," Dirkson replied before Bruce's words were out of his mouth. "Wait." He looked up at Susan and extended his hand impatiently. "Don't you want a notepad or something, Miss McCarthy, so that you can write this down?"

His demeaning attitude took her by surprise. Angrily she swallowed and said, "That's a good idea. I don't happen to have one with me."

Impatiently Dirkson walked to his desk, pushed a button on the intercom and spoke into it. "Miss Samuelson, bring us three, no, make it four notepads, some pencils and a few pens. Hurry with that, won't you? And where is Arthur? I told him to serve us coffee and tea as soon as he saw that we were all gathered. See that it's handled at once."

Susan listened to the man's arrogant delivery of his message. He probably treats everyone as patronizingly as this, she imagined. Everyone, that is, except people like Larry, Hal Mauldin and Bruce Powers. She decided she didn't like Evan Dirkson. There wasn't much there for her to like.

Vowing that she wouldn't be intimidated, Susan got up and walked around the room, giving the old-masters paintings a once-over while the others were being served by a breathless man who'd rushed through the door the moment Dirkson had switched off the intercom.

"Are you interested in coffee, Miss McCarthy?" From the head of the conference table Dirkson held up a cup and saucer.

"Yes, thanks."

The secretary brought in tablets, pens and pencils. Taking her time, Susan returned to her chair. Dirkson himself handed her a notepad with the initials E.D. centered on the top.

"Are we ready to begin?" Dirkson waited a second. "As you were saying, Bruce?"

"Well, I think—"

Dirkson seemed so anxious to get things going that he interrupted the star. "Do you want a fight scene? If you do, I think there's a perfect place on page thirty-six."

While the others turned to the page in their scripts, Susan kept her head down, her eyes on the blank notepad in front of her. She told herself to wait and see what would happen.

"People, I have been over this script again since we met yesterday, and I think I've also found a spot where we could have a wonderful chase scene. It could be done during one of the times the man's on a cocaine high." Evan looked to Bruce for approval.

Susan watched the two men interact. Bruce was saying very little and Dirkson was doing everything he could to please the star. She began to doodle on the notepad. Suddenly she was aware of Bruce watching her. She put down her pencil and looked straight into his eyes. They were amazing. They seemed hypnotic, enticing, mysterious. Despite her best intentions, she couldn't help but feel a certain magnetic twist way down low in the pit of her stomach. It disgusted her, but she felt drawn to the mystery in those smoky blue-black eyes of his. After a second or two, she drew her attention away.

She couldn't describe what that momentary look had cost her self-esteem. She ran her tongue over her lips and picked up her pencil again, starting to doodle once more, but this time in an effort to distract herself.

The man was too damned attractive for his own good—and for her own good, she decided.

"I wasn't thinking in those terms, Evan." Bruce picked up the movie script. "I thought about a couple of one-liners that we might add. On page fifty-six when he says . . ."

Susan listened to his voice. It was the same voice she'd heard in the movie theaters when she'd gone to see his movies and for a couple of hours had given herself up to the fantasy of this larger-than-life creature. No wonder she considered him a womanizer, she thought. He was probably crazy about women. He had probably never met a woman who didn't instantly succumb to his charms, and the man was loaded with charms. She watched the way the cleft in his chin moved as he spoke. She guessed it was the atmosphere around him that she didn't like. She didn't like the way everyone treated him as though he'd discovered the New World. It made her uneasy.

"Are you getting this down, Miss McCarthy?" Evan Dirkson stared pointedly at her notepad.

"I'm taking notes in my head," she answered in a dry voice.

"Do you agree with my suggestions?" Bruce Powers asked, and then watched as her expressive face turned into an indifferent mask. The first time he'd met her he'd been touched by the eagerness he'd seen in her light blue eyes, the intensity of her expression as she'd carefully thought out every comment before she'd spoken. Now her eyes looked lifeless.

"Yes." That was all she'd say. With her pencil, she began to scribble quick notes, bending down as if she couldn't see the paper too well. She'd promised herself she'd go along with them long enough to see in what direction they would try to go with her script. She hadn't promised to help them. If they wanted to tear it up, they'd get no help from her.

Hal Mauldin added a few suggestions that Evan agreed with and Susan quickly wrote down. Then Bruce was asking her again, "Do you agree with the suggestions so far?"

Damn him, she thought. Why couldn't he leave well enough alone? She ran her fingers through her curly hair, an act of frustration. Licking her lips, she looked at Larry. "Not particularly."

Evan Dirkson's head snapped up, and he gave her such a venomous look that she momentarily wanted to shrink down into the chair. Bruce's expression was dark: brows drawn, mouth distended. Hal Mauldin eyed her with what looked like amazement.

"Are you happy with this script now?" Evan asked, his eyes focusing solely on Bruce.

Susan kept her head down as though she were writing again, trying not to give her feelings away.

"Then shall we say it's a deal?" Evan's voice was full of relief. "Tomorrow, lunch at La Scala. We'll finalize our agreement with fresh fettuccine. What say?"

"I'll have my lawyers contact your people, Evan." Bruce stood and shook hands with everyone.

When he came to Susan he said, "I like your script, Susan. I really do."

"Then why not leave it as it is? It's a perfect script to challenge an actor. I think it's the kind of script that could make an ordinary actor into an outstanding one."

"Miss McCarthy, are you saying you don't want your script changed at all?" Dirkson interrupted.

"Yes, and I'm also saying that I think Mr. Powers could see this script as an opportunity to stretch himself. He could change his image entirely with this, or at the very least add a new one." Bruce Powers was her only hope.

"And if we insist on the changes we've discussed?" Dirkson prodded.

"Then I'm afraid I'll have to insist that my script remain unsold for the time being. I haven't signed the contract yet."

There was stunned silence in the room. After a few moments, Larry stood up. "Perhaps we should give you gentlemen time to think this over. I'll be in my office, Evan, until six o'clock." Hurriedly, he ushered Susan out of the still-quiet office.

Back at his home, Bruce Powers changed into sweatshorts and a sweatshirt. He went into his exercise room and began working on his rowing machine, straining hard, extending his arm muscles, out, back, out, back, until he could feel his muscles begin to protest. Then he began to pump harder, working up a sweat as he tried to push himself to the point of exhaustion. Exhaustion meant one didn't have to think. He didn't want to think.

But when he could stretch and pull no more, his mind was still going full tilt. He stared hard at his reflection in the floor-to-ceiling mirrors that covered the walls of the room.

Susan McCarthy—who was she? Why had she stirred up all these feelings inside him? And how? He hadn't said a hundred words to the woman. He didn't even know her.

But she'd made him think. Think about what kind of person he wanted to be. Think about what kind of actor he wanted to be. She was threatening—silently threatening. It was as if she were a scalpel and was slicing through all his posturing to expose the real Bruce Powers. He could feel her criticism of him, of his way of life.

He slung the oars on the rowing machine away from him so hard that they rocked loudly against the machine itself. He stood up and walked around the room, running his fingers across each of the pieces of equipment purchased to keep the star looking like a star.

Susan McCarthy had snapped at him at the wrong time in his life. That was it—that was the reason for his not being able to forget her or her hurting words. He was unhappy, had been for a while. Dissatisfaction had become a daily way of life. As a result, he walked around with a short fuse all the time. He got mad about nothing. He took everything the wrong way because there was no right way.

He had it all—fame, fortune, more women than any man had a right to, and he wasn't happy. It was a sad state of affairs for a man who'd come so far.

He was weak right now, he told himself. He was at a crossroads in his life. Maybe it was a midlife crisis. He didn't know. But he did know that when she looked at him he could feel her dissatisfaction, and he wanted to please her. He wanted her to look at him and like what she saw.

He went to the mirror and stared coldly at the image of himself. Everyone else saw the face, the body, the hair, the eyes, the mouth. Susan McCarthy had been looking beyond that; he'd sensed it right away.

Was that why he was attracted to her, he asked himself. Was that why he'd watched her so closely as she'd gotten up to walk around Dirkson's office? He'd found himself fascinated with the straight lines of her back, the narrow curve of her hip. He'd found himself wanting to trace them with his fingers. He'd imagined himself with her, holding her in his arms, taking her to bed. But that was ridiculous. Bruce Powers could have any woman he wanted. Why would he want her? He stared into the mirror.

Then he glanced up at the clock over the door and went to take a shower. His steps were brisk, the movements of a man with a purpose.

As he stood outside her hotel room door, he recalled how surprised Larry Steinem had sounded when Bruce had called him, asking where he could find Susan. Not any more surprised than he was himself, he thought. He knocked once, aware of adrenaline pumping through him, exactly as it had when he'd first set out years ago to make the rounds of the agents in Hollywood, hoping for a lucky break. It seemed to have been a long time since his adrenaline had pumped like this, but it felt good. He felt that his body and his mind were responding to it. He knocked a second time.

"Just a moment," she called, and his immediate thoughts were to get out of there as fast as he could. His heart was pounding, and he tried to laugh at himself. Imagine Bruce Powers, Dream Lover, nervous about talking to Miss Susan McCarthy from Amarillo.

When she opened the door, he grinned, as much to himself as for her benefit. In an instant, he realized she was a great deal more attractive than he'd been giving her credit for. Her face was without makeup and its paleness only made the widely rounded blue eyes more pronounced. Her lips were naturally tinted in shades of pink and as he watched her run her tongue across her lower lip he was attracted to the added shine. He was drawn back to her eyes; she gave him a look that seemed to be both angry and determined.

She took a step back. "What are you doing here?"

Ignoring her question, he leaned against the door frame and asked his own, the one he'd rehearsed as he'd driven his Maserati recklessly along the crowded streets to get here. "So you want to be a famous writer?"

She said nothing, merely looking at him, her eyes speaking for her. She kept one hand leaning against the wall and the other hand on the door.

"You're supposed to say, So you want to be a famous actor?" He flashed her one of his brightest smiles.

Silence.

"Well?"

Bruce gently pushed away her arm and stepped past her. "So maybe I'm already a famous actor. Maybe now I want to be a good actor."

She shut the door behind him, and he studied her reactions, taking in the way she'd looked defenseless for a second or two and then how her eyes, her entire body, had taken on a posture of stubbornness. Bruce found it all very appealing. She wasn't an actress who carefully planned her every look. She wasn't a woman who'd accustomed herself to manipulation. She was herself.

"I've been told there are drama schools all over the place out here. Why don't you try one?" She leaned against the door.

She was wearing a white silk blouse and the skirt to the suit she'd worn to the afternoon meeting, a simple straight purple skirt. The blouse was wrinkled, and she stood in her stocking feet, looking much smaller than he'd thought when he'd met her earlier. She had a pencil stuck over one ear and now he noticed a pair of glasses dangling from her hand as though she'd taken them off to answer the door. To him, she looked sexy and he didn't know why. If he were to describe her look to anyone else it might not seem so, but he found her arousing in a very special way.

"I don't want to go to drama school."

She folded her arms across her chest. "Well, what do you want, then?"

Susan couldn't help herself. In all her confusion she found herself looking at the way he was dressed, in a black silk shirt that looked handmade and precision-tailored slacks of oyster white. The man wore his clothes with a severely casual air, as though he remained always ready to have a national photographer capture his image for the public, yet at the same time his offhand elegance was coating over his innate sensuality. Bruce Powers's virility shimmered like a beacon on a lighthouse.

"I want to make your movie." He sat down on one of the two chairs in the room and looked over at the desk where she had a typewriter set up. "Are you working?"

"Yes."

"Working on the script?"

"Yes."

"But not changing anything?"

"No."

He began laughing. "For somebody who's so articulate on paper, you're a regular chatterbox in person, aren't you?"

"You're telling me."

He looked around the room. "Got anything to drink? It's toddy time in L.A."

She hadn't moved. From her place in front of the door, she stared at him, a long thoughtful look. Her eyes had a touch of green in them now, and Bruce thought he saw confusion hidden deep inside them.

A sigh escaped her lips. "What exactly do you want? Tell me, please."

He laughed again. "You don't like me very much, do you?"

"I don't have to. You like yourself enough for both of us."

His laugher was raucous. "Hey, that's a good one," he persisted. "You should write that down. You can use it in a script sometime."

Susan slumped against the door and then threw her hands up in the air. "I don't understand," she said. "Why are you here?" She moved her hands to her hips. "You're not exactly the one I might expect knocking at my door."

"Hey!" he yelled, jumping up from the chair. "You act like all this is my fault."

"Well, it is."

"Ridiculous." He felt his temper rising.

"It's ridiculous but it's true."

"Look, Susan, I've come here to talk to you because I believe that with a little bit of luck and a whole lot of patience, between the two of us we can make *Temptress* a contender."

A knot formed in Susan's stomach. "You won't get any argument from me about it."

"I've come to ask you a question. An important question. I hope you'll be honest with me."

"About what?" she asked, not trusting him.

"Do you believe I've got the talent for this part? Do you see me on the screen crying and screaming as a down-and-out addict?"

His words sounded so sincere that she looked at him for a long time. Then she gave her head a quick nod. "Yes, I do."

He walked over to the window and looked down on the people sitting around the swimming pool in the early evening twilight. She was more confused than ever.

"Now let me ask you a question. Why would you bother asking me? What value could my opinion possibly have to a man like yourself? I told you today what I thought."

He turned to gaze at her, and his eyes were dark with emotion. "Because I believe you love your script. I think you believe in it more than anything else right now. I saw your expression, the way you talked about *Temptress*. You love the script the way a man loves a woman." He stalked across the room and gripped her arms with both his hands. "I want the truth, and you're the only one I can trust to give it to me."

Wincing inwardly, Susan felt the first stirrings of sympathy. The man had everything, yet he was looking to a woman he'd barely met to give him guidance. Truth. How terrible that he had no place to go but her. How terrible for him.

He let go of her arm and walked over to the windows again. The knot in Susan's stomach began to unwind.

"I do love my script. The way I wrote it, not the way you and Mr. Dirkson are changing it."

"I made a serious film. I really tried to be serious once, but it didn't work."

"In *Rainy Days*?"

"You win the Kewpie doll." His tone became lighter. He was trying to kid around with her now. "It was 1976—my last dramatic role. It's fate maybe, but people like to see me driving a souped-up Chevy, drinking beer and cracking jokes."

"I want to ask you a question. You don't have to answer it if you don't want to. I'll understand."

He waited, aware of a tenseness running along his spine and the surprising feeling that he hadn't shared himself like this with anyone else in so long he couldn't remember. "Shoot, hoot. I'm all ears." He gave her a leering grin—one he was famous for using repeatedly whenever he substituted on *The Tonight Show*.

"No, I'd better not."

"Go ahead."

"No."

"Chance it."

"We're getting along too well."

"Go ahead. I won't get angry."

"Well, okay. What I was going to ask is, are you afraid of taking the chance on this movie? Are you afraid your fans won't like it or are you afraid you can't cut it?"

"Wheewee!" Bruce slapped one hand against his forehead. "Tell me, Miss Susan McCarthy, are all screenwriters so blunt?'' He swung around. ''You are one tough customer.''

''Not really,'' she said gently. She went to stand beside him. ''I just like the truth. Do you want *Temptress* to take on a comedic tone because you see the story that way or because you aren't comfortable with it as it is?''

The tone of her words reminded him of how he'd compared her to a scalpel. Well, one thing about it, he thought, she had laid his nerve center bare and exposed. He tried not to be bitter about it. She was a refreshing change from the hangers-on he had with him every day. He felt excitement swirl through him. If it was truth he was after, he'd certainly come to the right place.

''If I agree to do the movie as it stands, will you agree to work with me, talk me through it from start to finish about what you see the character...what's his name?''

''Lanny.''

''About what Lanny's motivations are?''

She nodded her head, amazed at what was happening between the two of them.

''I want an Academy Award, Susan.''

''Then let's do the movie with my original script.''

''Agreed. If you'll agree to what I asked.''

''Oh, Bruce, how wonderful!'' She could hardly believe her ears. It was really going to happen. *Temptress* would have its day on the screen. Overcome with joy, she flew into his surprised arms.

Uncertainly, he put his arms around her. He shut his eyes, taking in the flowering fragrance of her perfume, marveling at how light she felt when he embraced her. He savored the softness of her skin as her cheek grazed his own.

"This!" she exclaimed. "This is what I wanted all along." She started to step back, recovering from her shock.

He held her fast, unwilling to release his hold on her. He turned his head ever so slightly and brushed his mouth against the tender shell of her ear.

Caught by surprise, she tried once more to pull herself away. Her heart began to dance inside her chest and she felt a surge of dangerous emotion.

"Me too," he whispered as he held her fast and let his tongue approach her ear once, then again.

He felt her body begin to stiffen and knew she would be out of his arms at any moment. Suddenly he was covering her hair with kisses and then his hands held her face as though he would never let her go. He was trembling inside. The Dream Lover was trembling, he thought with surprise. His lips found hers, searching at first, then more commandingly as he let his tongue trace its way along her lower lip much as he'd seen her do automatically several times since they'd met. His hands were alive with feeling as they moved from her cheeks to weave a trail along her back, pulling her against him.

It wasn't an explosive kind of kiss, a no-holds-barred kind of kiss. She was glad for that. If it had all seemed too practiced she would have run away. Still, she hadn't planned on finding the kiss to be so intoxicating. Her legs went rubbery and her body felt as if it were on fire.

She brought her arms up to his shoulders to let her hands stray across his neck. She wanted nothing more than to test, to explore the feel of the man. His kiss intensified and she felt his tongue plunge inside her mouth, and suddenly Susan was being kissed in a way she'd never known was possible. The man was consuming her, drawing her tongue to his, taunting her, pulling from her the same kind of urgency that she could feel inside him. His body moved against hers seductively. He was overwhelming, demandingly so, and she felt as if she were powerless to resist.

He liked the way her mouth felt when it met his. He liked the feeling of holding Susan in his arms. She was going to be good for him. He knew it instinctively. She made him want something more out of his life. She made him quiver with desire. He couldn't remember being quite so taken with a woman like this before. She touched him on many levels.

As she responded to the warmth of his kiss, Susan talked to herself. She wondered if this humility of his was fake or real, planned or spontaneous. Then, as his lips worked their magic over hers, she began to wonder if this was real or only a dream. Could it be real, this fire that blazed inside her, the fire of sexual attraction? Could she allow herself to be caught up in the intimate arousal of having his body pressing against hers with a demanding message?

Could she handle this Dream Lover? Could she keep herself protected? She knew better than to let herself feel anything more than the headlong pleasure of being kissed by America's dream. Better to pull back, to stop this insanity before it went too far. She was acting out a fantasy, but she was afraid it was a self-destructive one. Susan had always known she was the sort of person who couldn't separate the physical from the emotional. She was sure Bruce Powers had been doing it for so long that he might not know the difference anymore.

"Please," she said. "Don't."

"It's all right," he said in a soothing voice.

But his words had come too quickly, too reassuringly, as if he'd spoken a stock phrase. She tensed and pushed away.

He reached out for her but she slipped from his arms. "I'd like you to go," she told him as she walked toward the windows.

"Susan." Bruce started for her.

"Now," she said coldly.

"Look, I was happy. I thought you were, too," he said defensively, confused by her abrupt change of heart. "I certainly didn't mean to offend you. I didn't mean anything by it, actually." He shook his head, suddenly unsure of himself.

"You didn't?"

She stared at him for the longest time and Bruce thought he'd never been under such scrutiny, not even when he'd stood in front of a close-up camera. How had this all gone so eerily wrong, he wondered.

"No, of course you didn't. I'm sure that's the way you handle all the women in your life. You get your way without ceremony, don't you?"

"I can explain, Susan."

"There's nothing to explain. Nothing of importance."

"Well, something sure as hell has gone wrong. One minute I'm holding you in my arms and the next minute you're cutting me to shreds."

"Let's just say I'm not used to Hollywood. I'm not used to this way of doing things. I feel manipulated."

"But I wasn't . . ."

"No, I can see that you didn't intend it. As you said, it meant nothing."

"That's not what I said, Susan."

"Good night, Bruce. Please make sure the door is closed tightly when you leave. I want no more intrusions tonight." She turned back to stare at the scene below her, her heart feeling heavy in these new surroundings of hers.

Chapter Four

At first he'd been caught up in a cold knot of fury. He was not accustomed to being rejected by a woman. He'd felt surprised at her gall and taken aback by her nerve. There was an entire town, a world full of pretty faces and willing bodies out there. And she'd pushed him away.

He'd gone home, put on a Sarah Vaughan tape and fixed himself a strong shot of good brandy. Three drinks later he'd managed to persuade himself that he'd misjudged her. She had challenged him with angry words, which he'd at first thought meant she couldn't stand him. But what she was trying to say, trying to do, finally dawned on him.

She was afraid of him. She was afraid of the mystique of Bruce Powers, the movie star. Everyone had read the trade papers' gossip columns, seen the reports done on him in magazines and on television. Susan had let herself become a victim of the hype.

His reputation as an Errol Flynn type had been gained through deliberate, carefully planned publicity. His publicist had traipsed to his door with one starlet after another, pushing him to be seen with a different girl on his arm every week. After a while, it had become easy. He didn't remember half their names or anything else about them. His evenings had blurred one into another, becoming unmemorable, yet the scheme had worked. His reputation as a lover was rock solid.

That was why Susan had behaved the way she did. She knew his reputation. She was afraid of becoming the next on his list. He couldn't believe it was anything else.

He didn't see her as he saw all the others. She was different. There was no chance of her disappearing into the bag of nameless faces and faceless names. He'd have to make her see.

When he'd satisfied himself that he was right, Bruce had turned out the lights and gone to sleep, knowing that he'd probably have a puffy face the next day from the alcohol. He'd have to try to do something about it before the luncheon at La Scala. There would be paparazzi everywhere and his picture would be out on the newswires before the luncheon was over. He took comfort in the thought that his dark glasses would probably do the trick. They could cover a multitude of sins.

The next morning, Johnny woke him with a glass of freshly squeezed orange juice, a bowl of Shredded Wheat, low-fat milk and a piece of dry toast. "Cook said I was to ask you if you're going to eat at home tonight."

Bruce sat up on the edge of the bed. "Put the tray on the table. It looks terrible."

"Yeah, but cook said you told her to count the calories and not go over three hundred for breakfast. You've had a call from Mr. Dirkson's office about lunch at one-thirty at La Scala, and your lawyer called. Said you're going to get whatever you want on the *Temptress* contract. Mr. Dirkson's guarantee."

Bruce nodded. "Where's my coffee?"

"Cook said you were trying to lay off."

"I was, but I changed my mind. How about one cup of coffee?"

"Sure." Johnny started out the bedroom door. "Big night last night?"

"What makes you think so?"

"A little puffy around the eyes." He went for the coffee.

Taking a drink of the orange juice, Bruce shook his head. This wasn't what he'd intended for himself when he'd started out in Hot Springs, Arkansas, wanting to go to Hollywood. He'd never given any thought to the narcissistic life. All he'd wanted was to get out of a neighborhood where the men took their lunch to work in a brown paper sack every day and came home dragged out from trying to make a living for their families on meager wages at mediocre jobs. He'd wanted more and his mother had encouraged him to go out and find it. When he'd gotten the lead every year in the high school plays, his mother and his drama teacher had been full of encouragement, telling him to go where people would appreciate his abilities. When he'd mentioned Hollywood, his mother had cried because it was so far away, but she'd helped him pack and talked his father into giving him money for a one-way bus ticket.

He'd come so far. Yet his ideas of what it would all be like were vastly different now than they had been in the past. If anyone had ever told him he'd be worrying about puffy eyes, he'd have plowed through that person's chin with his fist. But it was the truth. The name of the game in Hollywood was looks, and right now the younger the better. Men and women were being pushed aside by kids who weren't even out of high school being made up to look teasing and provocative. It wasn't a middle-aged game unless you were an actor, a real actor. Then you just might stand a chance.

"Boss." Johnny carried a single cup full of hot coffee on a wooden tray. He put the tray down on the edge of the table and handed the coffee to Bruce.

"Thanks."

"What do you want me to do for you today? You want a rubdown?"

Taking a sip of the fresh coffee, Bruce studied Johnny for a moment. Built like a Japanese wrestler, Johnny was a nice-looking jock who was as loyal to Bruce as any man could be. Johnny was always around. He followed Bruce's directions to the letter, and if he wasn't too bright, well, so what? He was as kind a man as they come, and Bruce liked that about him. He also knew that Johnny would never leave him. He was good to have around, and Bruce was as good to him as he knew how to be.

"I'm going to take a shower. I want you to send a dozen white orchids to Miss Susan McCarthy at the Beverly Hills Hotel. The card should read, 'Looking forward to working with you. Here's hoping the lady will accept apologies for last night. Love, Bruce.'" He hesitated. "Make that three dozen orchids and you personally deliver them, Johnny. I want to make sure she gets them before our luncheon meeting today."

Susan thanked the man who delivered the exquisite orchids and at the same time she studied his face. He seemed vaguely familiar, a face she recognized from the past few days.

She didn't know what she expected, but when she opened the card she couldn't believe what she read. Bruce was apologizing. It was something she'd hardly been prepared for.

When he'd stormed out of her hotel suite the previous night, he'd looked as though he wanted to kill her. Now his employee had shown up with an armful of expensive hothouse orchids and a card saying Bruce Powers was sorry.

No matter that she'd acted like the ingenue. She'd done the right thing. The way she'd gone about it might have been a little harsh, but she'd done the right thing. When she had felt his kiss making her legs go rubbery and setting her body on fire, she'd stopped it before things went any farther.

Bruce Powers's life was too full of easy women. She had no intentions of succumbing to his picture-perfect looks and his manipulations. Now his orchids and card told her she'd done the right thing. He hadn't really wanted her, either. He'd just been doing what was expected of him. A man of his reputation probably kissed every woman he was ever alone with, regardless of the circumstances. After all, she had been the one who had thrown herself into his arms. Her enthusiasm had made him think she wanted him. She almost smiled at the embarrassing memory.

After talking to Larry, Susan dressed for lunch at La Scala. Larry had told her that Dirkson wanted them to all have lunch together and that meant Dirkson wanted desperately to buy her script.

When Larry had explained that Dirkson was going full steam ahead as if work on the film would begin immediately, Susan felt a shimmer of apprehension flash down her spine. Everything was happening at once.

"This is the big moment, Susan. This is your contract." Larry handed it to her with a fatherly grin as he drove them to La Scala. "Dirkson sent it over by messenger, hoping you'd want so desperately to sell the script that you'd forget your objections from yesterday."

As she took the multipaged contract from him, Susan felt her breath catch in her throat. Was she really this close to grabbing the brass ring?

"Well, say something." Larry glanced over at her frowning face.

"I'm speechless. I'm enjoying every second of this, engraving it in my memory. Having a man like Dirkson come back a third time because of my script is a little overwhelming." With delicate moves, Susan gripped the contract. She tried to read it but the words blurred before her eyes.

"You should be." Larry shook his head. "I hardly believe it all myself, my dear, and I'm a man who's seen almost everything."

"Oh, Larry, it's all very tempting," she said, sighing. Looking out through the window, Susan read the highway signs for Santa Monica and Carmel. California, the land of pretend, she thought.

"Yeah, that's what he's hoping," Larry said with a rising voice.

She nodded, trying to read various sections of the contract. "Larry, there's a section in here about my going on location. I didn't realize it was so carefully spelled out in a contract like this."

"That's the funny part. When Dirkson called and said the contract was on the way, he said he'd added some of these things because Bruce Powers's lawyer had demanded it. Something's happened. I think Powers has changed his mind.''

Susan wanted to tell him about Bruce's visit, but she didn't know where she'd begin. After the way she'd behaved with him, she didn't think Bruce Powers would ever have another thing to do with her.

''The way Dirkson sees it, Powers intends you to be with him all the way on this thing. You're to be in all the meetings, you're to be there when all the scenes are shot . . . you're going to be involved from start to finish.'' Larry shook his head. ''That's the most unusual thing I ever heard of, especially for a newcomer. But Dirkson said Powers insisted, along with Powers's being the final approving authority on script changes.'' He looked over at her. ''Powers wants to have the final say on your script. If you still feel the way you did yesterday, I think we should just tell them at the end of lunch that you'll take your script elsewhere.''

Her mind traveled back to the conversation with Bruce. After a moment, she said, ''Last night, Bruce Powers came to see me. He said he'd be willing to leave the script alone.''

Larry gave a low whistle. ''So that's why all this has changed.''

''Well, I don't know, Larry. By the time he left, I'd made him angry again.''

Larry answered her with a laugh. ''We're about to find out,'' he joked, ''if you made him angry or not. I doubt that he'll be here if you made him too mad.

Here we are. La Scala." He turned the Mercedes into the restaurant parking lot.

Before they got out, Susan said, "You don't act too surprised, Larry. Why is that?"

"Because I could tell from the beginning that Powers was attracted to you. I may be an older man, Susan, but I'm not blind. Besides, you've got the best script around, and maybe, just maybe, what you said to him sank in."

The full-fledged elegance of La Scala was what she noticed first. Not that she hadn't seen places as fine. It was just that the atmosphere, the elegant-looking guests seated at the tables, everything put together, added up to create the perfect ambience.

Everyone else was already there when the two of them were seated. Bruce looked up at her with eyes that looked expectant rather than angry, and she found herself wondering what was going to happen between them today after last night's events.

The men stood up. "Sorry for our tardiness. I was held up at the office," Larry told them as he held the chair out for Susan.

Bruce decided that if he teased Larry a little, the group might relax with one another a little more quickly. "I'm glad you were, Larry." He gave the agent a jaunty grin. "It's helped my reputation." As they all laughed, he looked over at Susan once more.

When he saw that gentle smile of hers, he was reminded of how much she'd hurt him last night. It was something he'd never let show, especially when he'd made up his mind that he needed her. She alone was the person who could help him. He needed her strength, her innocent, absolute belief in her own work to help make his a success. It was obvious to him that she didn't understand his need yet, but in time she would come to. "Susan, I'm glad you came," he told her.

Susan thanked him, wanting to say something about the flowers, but feeling that her thanks should be done more privately. Aware of the way he kept looking at her, she felt her pulse surge. Turning her attention to the others, she tried to pretend that that intense blue-black look of his was having no effect. She knew she should be keeping her fingers crossed that Bruce's intentions were still to do *Temptress* as she'd written it, and not worrying about anything else that might be happening between them.

"Champagne," Dirkson was saying. "I've taken the liberty of ordering champagne for us. After all, we're here to celebrate."

He was seated across from her, dressed in an impeccable white linen suit with a black silk handkerchief in the pocket. All of them were dressed for the occasion. Evan Hal had on a royal blue sports jacket. Larry and Bruce were dressed in suits that had obviously been tailored to fit their bodies' every line. Larry sat across from Hal Mauldin, and Bruce was seated in the place of honor at the head of the table. Susan had worn a silk dress of pale violet, her last good dress. So far she'd worn every nice thing she owned in only three days. She made a mental note to call Louise and see if she was serious about going shopping.

Susan watched Bruce's reactions as two women approached the table, talking to the others with familiarity, never taking their eyes away from Bruce for long. When she was introduced to them, Susan was aware that they were sizing her up, as if for competition. It made her wonder if Bruce ever got tired of the constant attention. She'd like to be able to ask him about that part of his life, and many other things. She couldn't help but wonder if it was only her writer's curiosity that was leading her thoughts in this direction, or if there was a possibility that the memory of his kiss lingered in the corners of her mind like dusty motes that could not be easily swept away.

When the women had gone, the waiter brought a silver stand with iced champagne. Susan heard the name of the champagne spoken by the others with a respect obviously intended to show that it was a valuable vintage, but she decided her taste in fine champagne was something she'd have to work toward improving. This wine tasted no better than the extra-dry she bought from time to time at her local liquor store back in Amarillo.

Remaining quiet, Susan sat as an observer and, after the men had talked among themselves for a while, the waiter came to their table for their order. Bruce leaned his head in her direction, and she felt that tiny pulse in her throat rise once again.

"Susan, I recommend you try the abalone. It's wonderful." Giving her a nod of camaraderie, he turned back to Dirkson, who had been talking to him nonstop ever since he'd sat down. She watched him, aware that his concentration on Dirkson's monologue was wavering. She wondered what the next hour would bring to them both, and she felt stunned by his obvious friendliness. She didn't know whether to take it as a sign of something good or bad.

When the meal was served, Susan was still mostly quiet, responding to questions directed to her, but choosing the role of observer. The Hollywood give-and-take interested her immensely, and she enjoyed listening to the way these men used an underground communication system of sorts to deal with one another. As always, the conversation revolved around Bruce Powers. Bruce, she'd noticed, had remained quiet, letting the others carry on the conversation.

But when they were almost finished eating, Bruce cleared his throat and Susan looked up, her heart sounding in her ears as she wondered what he would say. Her future rested in his hands, and no one at the table was more aware of it than she was.

"After our meeting yesterday I've had time to think things over," Bruce said, looking intently around the table, into the eyes of each man and then coming to rest on Susan's.

"Good," Dirkson said. "What have you come up with?"

"I've decided I want to do the picture just as Susan's written it."

Dirkson's mouth curved downward, and then he allowed himself a smile of sorts. "Serious?"

"Serious."

"No, I mean, are you saying you don't want any car chases, that sort of thing?"

"That's right."

Susan saw Larry look over at her, a sly expression on his face. She tried to betray no emotion. The atmosphere at the table had suddenly gone cool.

"What about those one-liners you wanted? You don't want those?"

"No, I don't." Bruce looked directly at Dirkson. "I want it just like she wrote it. I want your commitment to go all out on this one. I want us to try and make it the best film in Hollywood this year."

Hal Mauldin started to laugh. "You're kidding, aren't you?" he asked through his laughter. "I thought we saw this thing the same way."

Susan's blood boiled. The intent of his words was that he didn't think as much of her script as Bruce did.

Coolly, Bruce eyed Hal. "I'm not kidding."

Dirkson broke in. "Okay, okay." He raised his hand in compromise. "You want to make a serious film, right?"

Bruce nodded.

Larry had already warned Susan that when the three men got into conflict, it was best for her and Larry to remain silent. This time she intended to follow his lead. Still studying them, she noticed how Bruce's commanding voice had taken on a trace of iciness, and it made her realize that he would be a hard man to fight, not just because he had clout, but because he was a strong man in his own right. She watched his jaw as it seemed to move forward a fraction.

"Then we'll make a serious film." Dirkson spoke in appeasing tones. "That was what we had intended in the beginning, anyway."

"But I think our ideas from yesterday were much better. I've been thinking about the car chases. We could add some funny things in here, some good scenes," Hal Mauldin said excitedly.

No one spoke. Bruce looked at Mauldin, sizing him up. Susan took a sip of her wine, and suddenly all eyes were turned to her.

"This is between you gentlemen," she said sweetly. "You already know what I think."

"Bruce, it's not a good idea," Mauldin began arguing. "You're good at comedy, light movies. This is a heavyweight script."

Bruce's eyes burned with anger. "And I'm not a heavyweight?"

"I didn't say that."

"You implied it."

"Naw, I just mean the public likes you funny. You said so yourself just the other day."

"But I don't want to make a funny movie right now. I want to make this one," Bruce shot back.

Mauldin's face had turned crimson. "So who talked you into this—Miss McCarthy here? What'd she do to get you to make such an abrupt about-face and go along with her?"

Bruce sprang from his seat and grabbed Mauldin by the throat. "Don't let me ever hear you talk like that again! Do you hear me?"

"Yeah." He moved away as Bruce's grip finally eased.

"Gentlemen, please. This is going to be in the papers tomorrow," Dirkson protested, fully aware of what bad publicity could do to a film before it had even begun.

"Apologize to the lady." Bruce spat out the words.

"I'm sorry, Miss McCarthy. It's just business, you know." Mauldin was adjusting his shirt and the lapels of his jacket. He turned to Dirkson. "Listen, Evan, I'm sorry." Perspiration stood out on his forehead. "I just don't want a flop. I'm too old to take the chance."

"A flop?" Bruce interjected. His voice was chilled, controlled. The undertone was one of rage.

"I...I don't mean it like that, Bruce." Mauldin couldn't look at him. He kept his eyes on the others. "I... Hell, man, listen to me. I'm trying to tell you that you don't know what the public wants if you think they want to see you up on the big screen crying and carrying on. This is a Jack Nicholson role. If we charge up the script, we've got a solid guaranteed hit. Why take the chance?" He looked to Evan for support, the perspiration beading solidly across the skin of his forehead.

Evan Dirkson leaned back in his chair, watching the two men. Mauldin's logic was right, Evan had no doubt, but Evan had no intention of doing anything to anger Bruce Powers. He'd studied Powers's income from his last four movies. Powers could make millions just walking across the screen, flop or no flop. He was money in the bank, and Evan wanted to make sure the money went into his own bank. Hal Mauldin could be replaced.

Bruce's mind was racing. He wanted to reach over and grab Mauldin by the throat again. His rage was volcanic. To keep himself from reaching out for Mauldin, he picked up his fork and clenched it in his fist. "Why don't you just butt out if it's too much for you, Hal? Give it up. Go make *The Return of the Little Rascals*. Give them a car chase. That ought to be your speed."

With careful attention to all his movements, Susan watched Bruce Powers. He was amazing. She hadn't dreamed there was so much emotion below the surface. She hadn't pictured him as the type who could exercise this forceful combination of control and strength. She couldn't control her own excitement as she wondered if he would be able to show this same feeling in front of the cameras. It was the type of fearlessness that her character in *Temptress* had.

"Yes, Hal, why don't you reconsider?" Evan asked.

"I..." Mauldin looked at Dirkson and then Bruce. "I just might," he said at last.

As the humiliation of Mauldin's words soaked in, Bruce told himself he would draw upon this experience, use it to further solidify his determination. He'd show Mauldin. He'd show them all—show the entire world. He was a talented actor. Bruce's eyes caught

Susan's. She'd help him, he told himself. She would help.

"All right, so Mauldin's out," Bruce stated flatly.

"I didn't say I was out, Bruce. I merely said I might consider it."

"Why not save us all the trouble of hassling this thing any further, Hal." Evan had studied Bruce long enough to know that Hal Mauldin had crossed a very important line with him. It would never do to have the star and the director at cross-purposes. "I'll find you another movie."

Hal flung his chair back, stood up and threw down his napkin. His mouth was white with tension. He opened it to speak, then changed his mind. Without another word, he marched out of the restaurant.

Nothing was said. Circumspectly, Evan motioned for a waiter to remove Mauldin's plate. When that was done, he looked at Bruce with raised brows. "Who would you like to direct this film?"

Bruce sat silently for a moment and then with the utmost sincerity, he said, "Me." He stared straight at Evan, his blue-black eyes never wavering.

Evan laughed, not too hard but with amusement. "Come on," he said.

"I'm serious."

"Bruce, you've never done anything like this before."

"I know that."

"But..." Dirkson took his gaze away from Bruce's. He was thinking of how much clout Bruce had. Sixty million dollars' profit on his last picture was nothing to sneeze at. He gave his shoulders a shrug. "If I let you do the directing, you'd have to do something for me in return."

Bruce leaned across the table. "What's that?"

"I'll pay you our agreed-upon fee for you to star in the movie, but you'd have to waive the directorial fee until it is determined that the movie can make back its investment."

"You're not asking me to give up my percentage of the movie's gross? That was agreed upon already."

"No. I'm saying you won't make a dime as the director until we find out if the movie's a hit or a miss."

"No. I think not. I think this picture can be great, Evan, and you'll have to pay me everything just as the contract's written and keep the director's salary in line with the codes and standards set by the Directors' Guild." Bruce reached across the table, waiting to shake Dirkson's hand, confident that he'd agree. "You see, Susan, this man is not above trying to take advantage of someone in a deal." He grinned. "If they'll let him."

Dirkson shook Bruce's hand, conceding to Bruce's demands.

Susan began to smile. Her future was looking brighter by the minute. Elation overwhelmed her as she realized she was going to have what she wanted. At the same time she told herself she'd seen something else in Bruce Powers's character today. He was a businessman who knew what he wanted and how he could get it. The depth of the man was surprising her at every turn.

"I have full control of this picture, right?" Once more, Bruce looked at Dirkson.

"Right. It's your neck." Dirkson smiled.

"I'll make it," Bruce told him, but his eyes were on Susan.

"Well, gentlemen, if it's all right with you, if all the excitement is over for the day, I'm going to have to get back to my office, where I can make my own deals." Larry stood up and then grinned. "Although I don't know when I've enjoyed myself more. Thanks for the lunch, Evan. Bruce, good luck on *Temptress*." They all shook hands.

Susan walked beside Larry as they hurried to his car. She heard someone calling her name.

"Hey, Susan."

She turned and saw Bruce running toward them. The coattails of his blue linen jacket were flapping behind him, giving her a glimpse of the muscular body she'd seen pictured in so many magazines over the past few years.

"Listen, I want to take you to dinner tonight. We can talk about the movie."

Larry walked on ahead of them and asked for his car. Susan took her sunglasses from her purse and put them on to block out the bright rays of the afternoon sun while she stalled for time.

"Uh . . ."

"Susan, I hate to break up your conversation but I have a three-thirty appointment," Larry called when the car was delivered.

"Maybe some other time," she said. "But thanks for everything you did for my script today." It was the first time she'd looked up at him. He was standing uncomfortably close.

"I'll call you, okay?"

"That's fine," she answered and hurried into Larry's car.

As he drove her back to the Beverly Hills Hotel, she listened to Larry's exclaiming over the unusual happenings of the day. She was full of a strong sense of well-being, knowing that Bruce intended to bring her script to life. She didn't understand the man. Not at all. After last night she'd expected him to hate her, to lash out at her either in person or through the negotiations. Instead he'd acted as though they were intimates, and that didn't sit well with her at all. She knew she couldn't handle dealing with him again, not when she was still so involved with the memory of how she'd felt in his arms. It wouldn't do to let herself dwell on the impossible. And she tried to tell her heart that same thing all the rest of the way to her hotel.

Chapter Five

Bruce had Johnny drive him home, where he changed into jeans and a knit polo shirt. He gave Johnny the night off, sent his secretary home early and left a message for the housekeeper that he wouldn't be eating at home but he'd like to have a fresh pot of Amaretto coffee made around 10:00 P.M.

He went out to his garage and walked around all the cars he had parked there, the Rolls, which Johnny loved to drive, his Mercedes, the Maserati and his old Triumph Spitfire. The Triumph was the first car he'd bought with part of the proceeds from his first screen role. He'd played the skirt-chasing son of a rum runner. The movie had been terrible, but it had given

Bruce plenty of opportunities to take off his shirt, and as a result he'd gained public attention right away.

Bruce took out the keys to the Triumph, carefully detached the cloth cover and put it away. It was going to be too pretty a California night not to drive the convertible.

Like a homing pigeon, he drove straight to the Beverly Hills Hotel and knocked on her hotel room door, not bothering to call ahead of time. She answered the knock in a white hotel robe, her hair wrapped becomingly in a towel turban.

"We've got to stop meeting like this," he teased.

She managed a smile. "You're absolutely right. I don't enjoy being caught looking like a walking wreck, especially out here in the heart of Beautyland. I'll bet you haven't seen a woman without makeup since you left . . . wherever you're from."

He laughed knowingly. "How about a lovely drive down the Pacific Coast highway, a juicy hamburger and all the conversation you can bear?" He gave her a convincing smile.

"I'm not dressed," she insisted.

"I'll wait." He glanced inside her hotel room. Feeling her resistance, he added, "Downstairs, in the bar. Come down when you're ready."

"Well, I . . ."

"It'll be fun. You'll see things you've never seen before."

She gave him a nod that said she'd go but she wasn't crazy about the idea, then she started to close the door. "Hey," she called as he walked down the corridor.

"I've been wanting to tell you thanks for the orchids."

"You're welcome," he answered with a wave of his hand.

She shut the door and collapsed against it. *I must be crazy,* she thought. How could she possibly think she could handle Bruce Powers? She'd said yes when she'd intended to say no.

When she stepped out of the elevator, Bruce was walking toward her. Immediately she became aware of the way people were staring at him, even inside a hotel where celebrities came by the dozens. She couldn't dismiss the uncomfortable feeling when he took her by the arm and led her outside to his car. As she heard people whispering Bruce's name, she shivered. Living in a fishbowl wasn't something she thought she'd like.

"I hope you don't mind having your hair blown," Bruce said when he helped her into the Triumph. He stood above her, looking down before he leaned over so that his words fell close to her ears as he teased. "You don't strike me as the type who'd worry about something like that."

"No," she said, smiling at him. "I don't mind at all. Besides, after a comment like that one, I wouldn't argue even if I did mind."

He laughed, then went around to the other side of the car and was helped in by one of the attendants. "Let's drive out to the coast highway."

Susan was watching the attendant who'd remained near the car. The young man hadn't taken his eyes of Bruce.

Bruce saw her staring, then turned his head to see what she was looking at. He saw the attendant reach for a pen inside his shirt pocket.

Hesitantly the attendant handed Bruce the pen and a piece of wrinkled paper he'd found in his wallet. "Would you mind, Mr. Powers? You're my idol."

Bruce nodded. "Sure, but have they changed the rules here or something? I thought anyone working here who did this was automatically fired on the spot."

The yound man blushed. "No...sir," he stammered. "I could get fired, but you're my idol and it would be worth it."

Bruce signed his name with a flourish and handed the paper and pen back to the attendant. "Whatever you say," he said before driving off. As he shifted the gears of the Triumph, he glanced over at Susan. Seeing the serious expression on her face, he wondered what she was thinking but knew that the odds were against his finding out. She struck him as the type of woman who revealed very little of herself. In Hollywood, he thought, that was probably just as well.

"How do you like it so far?"

"Los Angeles?"

"Yeah."

"I like it, I guess—what I've seen of it, anyway. I've only been here three days and they've been busy days. Maybe when I move out of the hotel I'll feel more in touch with things." The wind picked up her hair and rearranged it around her face in curly tangles. She lifted one hand up and brushed away the strands that had flown across one corner of her eye.

"When I first came here I hated it," Bruce was saying. "I wanted to be here, all right, but I hated how there aren't any seasons. The damned sun always shines, if you can see it through the smog." He smiled when he heard her laugh and increased his speed. He could smell the ocean, and he wanted to spend the evening with her at his side as he drove along the beach.

As he made idle conversation, Susan found herself becoming more at ease. Bruce might be a star, but when they were alone she was finding him as easy to talk to as anyone else.

"So tell me about yourself, Susan." He was having to shout now as his fast driving kicked up the wind. "I want to know about Susan McCarthy from Amarillo, Texas."

"Oh, there's not much to tell," she answered.

"Hey, come on. You're not going to tell me that you haven't led an interesting life. How can you call yourself a writer?"

"Not all writers have led interesting lives. Some of them have only thought about doing so. Their imaginations have done the rest."

"Then tell me about yours." He was filled with curiosity about her. Early on he had realized that he knew very little, and now when he looked at her, he couldn't help but wonder where she'd gotten this veneer of strength that seemed so integral a part of her.

She impressed him as a woman who knew herself better than anyone else.

"Let's see. My father was a cotton farmer and until I was twelve we lived on a farm twenty-one miles from town. I have a younger sister who lives in Amarillo and is dying to come to Hollywood. I expect to see her on my doorstep at any moment—when I get a doorstep, that is." Susan laughed, thinking of her sister, Sandy. "My father lost his farm because of a three-year drought and when we moved to Amarillo, all of us went to work trying to make a living. I've been a waitress, a secretary and a clerk in a department store. I worked my way through junior college and then my father got sick, so I've spent the past few years working as a legal secretary, helping my mother take care of my dad and writing when I could work it in. Writing has always been my first love." She thought hard for a second. "I take that back. Reading is my first love."

"Sounds like you've had a busy life."

If any other show-business personality had said this, she might have thought the words sounded patronizing, but coming from Bruce, the remark seemed sincere. He'd listened with great interest. "Busy but dull by most people's standards."

As the time passed, they found that they never lacked for conversation. Bruce asked more about her family and Susan told him as much as she thought he wanted to hear. Then it was his turn. He told her about his mother's belief in him and about how grateful he was that she'd lived long enough to see him become a star.

A full moon shone down upon them as they traveled along the highway, and despite the traffic, the people and the signs of civilization, Susan couldn't resist the feeling that they were alone together, shut away by an invisible barrier from every intrusion. She alternated between observing his perfectly formed features and the magnificent beauty of the reflected lights on the darkened ocean. Being with this American legend was like a dream.

"Are you hungry?" he asked after they'd been driving for an hour or so.

"Mmm...I suppose I am." She hadn't given much thought to food. She'd been too busy enjoying herself.

"There's a place a little farther down the road where they serve a good greasy hamburger and the best fried onion rings I've ever put in my mouth. It's not fancy but nobody bothers me there, either. Believe me, Tony's Place is about as far off the celebrity trail as anyplace I know."

She felt his eyes on her and turned to look at him. His expression seemed inviting, friendly, almost vulnerable. His eyes were sparkling, and his mouth was curved upward in a smile that conveyed something...something special, she thought before looking away.

"I'm glad you came with me, Susan. It's been a long time since I was with someone as easy to talk to as you."

Her reaction was slow in coming. She wanted to be friends with this man. He evidently wanted the same thing. But that was all she wanted, her mind insisted. That was all she could afford. He was the most sexually attractive man she'd ever been close to.

"I'm enjoying myself, too, and I guess I should apologize for last night while I'm at it. Not for what I said. I meant most of it, but for the way I said it, I apologize," she stated without looking at him. Instead she directed her gaze to the ocean, all the while telling herself that her pulse shouldn't race the way it was doing and her mind shouldn't dwell on the deep cleft in his chin.

"There's plenty of time to talk about all that," Bruce answered. "Not tonight."

From the outside, Tony's Place didn't look like much. From the inside, it looked even worse. Tony's Place consisted of a low-roofed, shingle-sided building with a front door that looked as if it had been kicked in once or twice. The inside was dimly lit and had old wrought-iron tables and chairs with the paint peeling off and a tiled floor that had no tiles left unbroken. Bruce led her through the building, obviously familiar with the place, and soon they were seated at a small table for two out on a patio that overlooked the ocean.

When the owner saw Bruce, he immediately had two men come out and move the few remaining tables and chairs away. The two of them were left all alone with a single candle under the stars.

"I bring you what you like," the owner said as he approached them carrying two brown bottles of Mexican beer. "You be wanting the usual?"

Bruce introduced them, then said to Susan, "What about it? Want to try that hamburger?"

She nodded, still trying to push back the tangle of hair the wind had whipped so destructively.

When Tony was gone, Bruce said, "It's not much, but I like it here."

Susan looked around. Everyone else had disappeared. There was only the sound of the ocean lapping on the shore, the semidarkness and the two of them. The air smelled of salt and moisture. She took a deep breath and closed her eyes. "I think I'm going to like it, too."

While they ate, they talked about movies. Susan found to her surprise that they seemed to like many of the same ones. She was also surprised that Bruce seemed to enjoy many of the books she mentioned as her favorites.

"How on earth do you have time for reading?" she asked, intrigued.

"You've never been on a movie set, I can tell. Half the time the star sits around waiting for the scene to be set up. I always have a book in my hand."

She could picture him sitting in a director's chair, with everyone walking reverently around him, trying hard not to disturb the star. She could imagine him absorbed in a book, oblivious to what was going on around him.

Outside, there were three not-so-young women standing around the Triumph. "Hey, Bruce, how about an autograph?" one of them said.

"Maybe some other time," he told them. He tried to smile as he glanced back at Tony's Place.

The roughest looking of the three spoke up. "No, now," she hissed as she leaned back against the driver's side of the door. She pulled out a pen and raised her skirt to expose the top of her thigh. "Right here."

As graciously as he could, Bruce moved her aside, then hopped into the car. Within seconds he had the car started and was backing out.

Susan could hear the insults being hurled in their direction. "Is that common?"

"Not at Tony's. One of the waiters must have told them we were there." He hesitated. "But it's not unusual, Susan. In fact, this was a mild encounter with my fans compared to some, and amazingly enough the women are usually the worst."

"Groupies, you mean? I've never seen anything so disgusting in my life." It had been a bizarre scene, one that left her feeling squeamish.

They were driving back to L.A. Bruce could feel Susan's tension. She hadn't liked what she'd seen.

"There are plenty of groupies around, although the musicians are the ones who have the most trouble with them."

"I'd hate it. It would almost be enough to make me want to forget the opposite sex." She watched his reaction. The incident hadn't seemed to faze him even though she'd found it absolutely sickening.

He looked at her and flashed her a grin that was intended to make her feel better. "It's a fact of life. Part of the business. Forget it."

She tried hard to match his smile, but her mind was going in a thousand directions again. How could anyone consider a life like his to be normal? And what kind of woman would feel comfortable with being forever in his shadow? He was intriguing, all right, but with a man like him, a woman would always have to feel she was playing with fire.

For the remainder of the drive, they said very little. When they had turned off the major thoroughfare and were traveling through a residential section, Bruce spoke up. "I want you to see my house."

"Tonight?" She hadn't even considered the possibility.

"Yes. I want to show it to you, give you a cup of coffee, a little more conversation and then I'll return you safe and sound to your hotel." He was smiling.

"Okay." What harm could there be in going to see his home, she asked herself, but there was an insistent fluttering inside her. The thought of going to his home gave her a sense of intimacy that she knew she wasn't going to deal with very well. Already she felt more tense.

Five minutes later they were turning into a paved drive that led to a high brick fence. Bruce pulled up to the tall iron gates and took out a plastic box from his glove compartment. "Computer operated," he explained. After he punched a coded series of numbers into the signal box, the gates opened and he drove through.

As she heard the gates close behind them, Susan looked around her. It was like being in wonderland. On either side of the drive were lavishly planted gardens that had a look of permanence, as if they had always been there.

When they came to the Tudor-style house, Susan could only stare. The house seemed to run on and on in two-storied splendor. She'd never seen anything so magnificent. There were no words to describe the immensity of the place, the blatant richness, the solid feeling of well-being. It was breathtaking.

They were greeted at the door by a man dressed in a white jacket and black dress trousers. Bruce ordered coffee to be served in the library and then dismissed the man while Susan busied herself looking at what she could see of the house. The entrance was two stories, with a stone staircase leading to the floor above and an iron-gated elevator directly behind the staircase. She tried to take it all in—the brightly colored Oriental rugs on the stone floor, the gold-leaf framed paintings hanging from each wall and the finely polished Elizabethan furniture along the walls.

"Bruce," she said, sighing, "this is the most beautiful home I've ever seen."

He gave her a smile that was a healthy combination of pride and boyish shyness. "Thanks. I think it is, too."

He led her into the library and poured the rich Amaretto coffee into two cups. When she expressed her pleasure, he took her by the hand and led her through the downstairs rooms, insisting that she bring her coffee cup along with her.

Susan found herself enjoying the way he was guiding her, stopping in each room to describe pieces he himself had found or to tell her about the remodeling of the house. It had once belonged to a famous silent-screen star, and when he'd bought it, the Tudor mansion had required a thorough renovation from the ground up.

Like two children caught up in a make-believe tale, they traipsed through the rooms, going back to the library for coffee twice before he led her outside to see the tennis court and the swimming pool. The pool was one of the largest she'd ever seen. There were stone carvings along the brickwork that lined the edge of the pool and a cabana that was large enough to house a family itself. The lighted tennis court looked as though it hadn't been used, and Bruce explained that he'd recently had it resurfaced.

When they returned to the main house, Bruce took her hand once more, and after they'd put down their cups of cold coffee, he led Susan up the stairway, stopping only long enough to tell her about his paintings. The names of famous artists escaped his lips faster than she could keep up with them, and Susan marveled at the value of the collection on the walls.

His bedroom was the most masculine part of the house she'd seen. His bed was huge, far oversized, larger than any king-size she'd ever seen.

"Did you have this specially made?" she asked.

"Yes. That's something I'd always wanted to have—room enough to sleep without ever feeling the edge of the bed." Bruce laughed at himself as he leaned an arm against one of the ornate mahogany bedposts. "I guess it comes from having to share a bed with a brother when I was a real little kid. I like to have plenty of room now."

Looking around at the room that could house five or six people comfortably, she made an observation. "I don't think you have anything to worry about."

"No," he said with another laugh. "I guess I don't. Now all I have to do is worry about filling it up."

She was standing in front of one of the floor-length windows, and when he spoke she looked at him. His smoky eyes held hers, and she felt an invisible connection weave between them. She turned back to the window.

"Well, I suppose I must go now, Bruce. It's getting late." Now that she'd ventured into this man's private world, she wasn't sure how to leave it. She was overreacting to him but felt at a loss to stop it. The only thing to do was to remove herself from the situation as quickly as possible.

"I was hoping you'd want to stay." He walked over to her and ever so gently settled his hand across the warmth of her back.

The thought of how and where he was touching her reminded Susan of two lovers from antiquity, comfortable with each other, enjoying passing their days together.

She felt her breasts respond, her blood swirl. She felt a racking pang of excitement so overwhelming that it pushed all other sensations away. The casual contact was too much for her to handle.

"I think not. Thank you for a lovely visit, though," she said as she extracted herself and started for the hallway.

"I want you to stay," he called out, and his baritone voice rolled across the room to her, seemingly building up energy as it traveled to her.

She turned back to look at him. He remained where she had left him, his hand still held out as if waiting for her return. "Bruce...no, thanks," she said, giving him a quick smile. "I really need to go."

Momentarily, he was at her side, moving with unexpectedly smooth strides that ate up the distance between them. "Please say you'll stay. You were wrong about me last night. In the past, I haven't tried to deliberately manipulate women to get what I want. They were the ones after me." His voice became lower, huskier. "I haven't been told off by a woman since...since maybe never. When I kissed you last night, it had nothing to do with manipulation. It had to do with how I felt, how you made me feel."

"I never intended this to..." She faltered, realizing now how he must have assumed she had planned on this happening.

"I did," he answered as his hand began to glide along the curve of her chin. He turned his hand around and brushed his knuckles against her cheek, then let them graze softly against the silken skin of her lips.

"Let's not spoil a lovely evening," Susan tried to say, but as she spoke, her lips moved against his knuckles and she saw his eyes brush to a close and then open wide to gaze down at her with an intensity that seemed more real than any words.

"I agree. Let's not," he said as he brought his lips down to settle gently against hers. He moved his hand to cup the back of her neck and immediately his lips moved more insistently against her own.

She tried to pull her mouth away. When he wouldn't let her, she spoke against his lips. Her words came out in muffled protest. "No, I'm serious."

Now he had wrapped his other arm around her waist so that she was engulfed in his embrace without hope of easily getting away from him. His lips were still moving against hers, and even as she tried to deny him access to the warmth inside her mouth, she could feel his tongue move insistently against her teeth.

He moved his head back a fraction and answered her with a cloudy look in his blue-black eyes. "I think I am, too, Susan. Don't ask me why, but I think I'm very serious." He breathed huskily as he bent to brush his lips across the arch of her neck.

She turned her head, trying to deny what was happening between them. Inside her chest, her heart was moving in a wild, erratic rhythm. She felt his hand snake up to grasp her chin so he could kiss her once more, and even as she braced her hands firmly against his chest in an effort to show her resistance, she was letting her lips do her talking for her.

He pulled away from her for a second, dropping his hands down to his sides. She stared into eyes that spoke of capturing the moment, eyes that promised something of an adventure.

Then Bruce bent and kissed ever so gently, barely a whisper of a touch—once, twice—before taking her face in his hands and pressing his mouth against hers. He ran the tip of his tongue in the space between her lips, teasing with gentle probes until at last he could feel those lips beginning to part and allowing him to gain entry and continue his exploration.

She reached up to grip his shoulders, clinging to him, a woman torn between the wanting and the knowledge that the kisses that seemed so perfectly tormenting were a credit to his practiced skill. Yet she wasn't able to overcome the power of his caress, the feeling of wanting more. She shut her eyes tightly, as if by doing so she could hold back the logic that her opened eyes would make her see.

He pressed her body against his as he let his tongue plunge hungrily into the warmth behind her teeth. He could feel her breath as it collided with his, a trace of sweetness, and he could taste her as his tongue followed the hollow of her cheek.

Breathlessly, Susan continued to give in to the arousal of his kiss. She let her hands begin to caress his powerful shoulders and when she felt his hands move away from her face and begin a slow journey downward to her breasts, her waist and then to curve along her backside until he was running his hands in sweeping circular motions around her buttocks, each swirling touch, each mesmerizing movement geared to urge her supple body nearer to his.

After a few moments, she could feel the hard contours of his thighs and the demand of his manhood as he pressed closer and closer, his mouth fastened to hers, his body enflaming hers. He let his hands glide upward along her back, ensuring their connection from breast to thigh. She felt as if she were attached to him. She could feel all that he was, all that was his.

Her fingers threaded their way along his shoulders and up the column of his neck. She thrilled when she heard him moan as his lips trailed down into the hollow of her throat, and his hands traveled back to her buttocks.

Then his hands were moving again, upward this time, until he found the hem of her sweater and moved it so that he could slide his fingers inside to make gentle contact with the warmth of her skin. His mouth began to move again to hers and this time, when his tongue entered her, she felt a new dimension of urgency, of need.

She was breathing deeply, rapidly. She felt him unfasten her bra and then she felt his hands cupping her breasts in a warmth that made her feel it was almost too hot, too unbearable. She quivered as his fingers sought out her nipples and on finding them, drew them to rigid life with delicate friction. She gasped.

"I want you to spend the night," he told her as he began to guide her toward the bed.

"No," she begged.

"Please." As he talked, he continued moving them toward the inviting softness. "I want you. I want to hear you say you want me."

When he had her near the bed, he abruptly picked her up in his arms and placed her down, settling his body gently on top of hers. He smiled at her and his smile was warm.

She felt the way his body fitted so perfectly with hers, felt the demands of his body as he lay across her. She knew that her own body was full of desire and longing; she ached with it.

"Please, Susan, I want you."

"I can't—I can't, Bruce." She opened her eyes and shook her head in an emotion she realized as despair. "I'm not the kind of woman whom you're accustomed to. I can't go in and out of your bed or any other man's."

She was shaking with the explosive combination of conviction and passion. It was terrible to have them at odds this way, inside a body that was on the verge of being lost, given up to the provocativeness of a man who had the ability to bring new meaning to the art of lovemaking.

"Oh, Susan," he cried as he held her face in his hands and brushed his lips tenderly against the peak of her nose. "Don't."

"It's not my style, Bruce."

"It's not a question of style, not with us," he whispered as he kissed the corners of her lips with soft butterfly kisses. "This isn't anything like what you're thinking."

His kisses made her want to dismiss her logic as the ravings of an old woman gone mad, but there was a nagging thought in her head. "What makes it different?"

"Because it's you and me," he told her, his voice still in a whisper, his lips working against her mouth and her resistance. He let his hand roam down along her body once more, as if he were on a discovery cruise.

She pushed him away, her hands shaky, but growing in strength. "I can't. I'm sorry."

"I want you, Susan." He waited for some reaction, but her eyes were cold and her body had become tense.

He rolled over and watched her as she got up from the bed and began straightening her clothes. He could still taste the honeyed sweetness of her lips, but now there was a new taste inside him—a taste of unfulfilled longing.

"You don't really want me. You want something you think I can do for you. You're just playing the expected part. I know that, Bruce."

Her words tore into him. She was talking about his image. Not the real Bruce Powers. The public invention.

"You're like everyone else. You see what you want to see." He shook his head in disgust. "Give me a little credit, Susan. I'm not as low class or as crass as you and the gossipmongers believe.'' He was taking jagged breaths. Having her reject him like this hurt him. ''Go on, then. I'll have Johnny drive you home.''

He went to the intercom and then whirled around. ''Damn it, I'll have to drive you. Johnny's gone.'' He hardly looked at her as he stormed through the bedroom door. ''Come on.''

The drive back to the hotel was the longest ride of her life. Silent. Hurtful. Mean. Lonely.

He drove up to the front of the hotel and jerked the Spitfire to a jarring halt. She barely had time to get out of the car before he had started up again, grabbing the door with one hand and slamming it shut, never looking back as he left a trail of smoke and sadness behind him.

Chapter Six

Susan, Susan." Bruce was shaking her by the arm. "We're coming into Santa Fe now." The noise of the jet swelled around them, and she felt the plane begin its descent.

She opened her eyes to look up at him. He was still sitting across from her, only now he'd taken off his jacket and was sitting on the edge of his seat. He let his hand run down the length of her arm before pulling it slowly away, and she was aware of the tingling trail his touch had left behind.

She looked over at the other two men. They were both watching her. "I suppose I must have slept," she said to them, half-apologetic.

"Yes, well, you also must have been dreaming, Miss McCarthy," one of the men whose name she'd immediately forgotten told her. "Your sleep didn't seem to be a comfortable one." He gave her a kindly smile.

"Maybe it's the altitude," Bruce said, sliding back into his seat and fastening his seat belt. "You'd better buckle up." He pointed a finger at her open belt.

She looked down. Strange, she thought. She didn't remember having unfastened it.

"I unstrapped your seat belt when the pilot gave us permission," Bruce explained, his eyes moving everywhere rather than meet hers directly.

She tried to smile, but she could feel her mouth resist. "Thank you."

Still feeling the effects of his touch, she thought back over her immediate problem. Susan had come to Hollywood with a host of misgivings, and things had happened far too fast. It wasn't enough that she'd moved to a new place, been plunged immediately into a situation in which she was wrestling with some of the most influential people in Hollywood over a script she believed in more strongly every day, but she'd become involved with the Dream Lover, the symbol of American masculinity. He'd rendered her more vulnerable than even the great Dream Lover himself knew, and there was nothing she could do about how she felt.

It was a little like walking into a darkened cave with no light source. She didn't know what to expect, and she had no way to protect herself. She only knew she was a woman filled with fear and she had good reason—very good reason.

Their landing was uneventful. So much so that she'd barely had time to look around at the beautiful land nestled snugly inside a valley, protected by mountains on all sides. They'd immediately been whisked into waiting station wagons at the airport and taken to the La Fonda hotel, a stuccoed building that Susan found enchanting.

When they were walking up the hotel stairs to their assigned rooms, Bruce had said, "Let's meet back here for cocktails and dinner at seven. We'll talk about our living arrangements then." Once again his eyes had barely connected with hers. Instead he'd focused on the two business companions. It was then that she'd decided that if he wanted to continue this show of indifference, it was all right with her.

After a shower and a brief rest, Susan went downstairs and wandered through the heart of the city. The buildings were beautiful reminders of the missions of the long-ago settlers. Around the square she saw the native Indians selling their wares, mostly silver and turquoise jewelry. She sat on a bench in the center of the square and closed her eyes, basking in the sunlight. When the sun went down she felt the air turn chilly, but she remained as long as she could. Being alone there was proving to be the most pleasant part of her day, and besides, she thought, it kept her from facing an uncertain evening.

At dinner that night she was mildly surprised that Bruce arranged to have her seated next to him, yet it hardly seemed worthwhile. He paid little attention to her. Mostly he spent the time talking to the others. A curly-haired, fast-talking man in charge of preproduction, named Julian Edwards, had joined them. He was the one responsible for making the location arrangements, including leasing the place where they would be staying. Susan had assumed that they would live at the hotel, but she soon heard Bruce telling Edwards what he wanted.

"Tomorrow I want someone to get me a house. I don't want to stay here."

"You don't like it here?" Edwards asked.

"It's not that. I'm going to be working at a very fast pace, under what I would imagine will end up being tough circumstances. This movie is going to be special." He looked over at Susan. "I need someplace away from everyone else."

"All right," Edwards answered. "I'll take care of it. Any particular house you have in mind? I mean, how many bedrooms do you want and all?"

"When will the rest of the crew get here?"

"I don't know. The end of the week, maybe. Mr. Dirkson is trying to get everything done as quickly as possible. He said you wanted to start like yesterday."

Bruce nodded. "I want four bedrooms. There will be Miss McCarthy, Johnny, my secretary and myself. Also, make sure there's help hired to take care of things. I guess if you could get a five-bedroom house that would be okay, too."

"Pardon me," Susan interrupted. "Why are you including my name in this? What's wrong with my staying at the hotel?" She wasn't certain she understood anything about making a movie, but she didn't see why she'd have to stay anywhere near him.

At first he ignored her. Then she said it again. "Why are you including me in this?"

"Rehearsal," he replied, drawing out the word as he spoke. "We have to rehearse. There are going to be many hours of rehearsal required. We need to be together."

The importance of his words fell on her like a meteor shower. "But—"

"That's the only way to do it." He glanced away from her. "Why don't you see about getting another house nearby?" he told Julian. "We can put my co-star in there, and a few other key people. That way we can all be near one another. We'll probably rehearse in the house you rent for me, provided it's large enough."

Fields gave him a nod. "I think it makes good sense."

"I don't," Susan complained. "Not for me, anyway."

Bruce glared at her, then said to the others, "Gentlemen, will you excuse us for a moment?" He stood and pulled her chair back for her, then took her by the arm to an empty corner table.

"Look, Susan," he began without really looking at her, "I told you before what the deal would have to be if I turned your script into a movie. Now I'm banking on you to cooperate.''

"I want to cooperate," she answered him. "I just don't see why I need to stay in the same house with you." Her eyes swept over his face, searching for some sign that would make her understand why he was treating her the way he was.

He read the confusion in her face. It only served to remind him how he'd felt the night she'd rejected him. "It's best this way. If I need you, you'll be available." He took his hand from her arm, and for the first time his eyes met hers. He started to turn away before he added, "Don't worry. You won't be bothered again. Not by me, at least." Pausing, he thought for a moment and then said, "It's strictly business. Both of us trying to make your script come to life."

Embarrassed, hurt, torn by a wave of conflicting feelings, she felt the blood pounding in her temples. "That's exactly the way I like it," she snapped.

He got up and returned to the others. There didn't seem to be anything else to be said between them.

Over the next few days, more and more people began to arrive from Hollywood. Julian Edwards searched for a house that would meet the star's standards, and on her first location trip, Susan analyzed everything, paying particular attention to watching Bruce in operation. It was obvious that his role as director demanded much more than that of a star. The center of attention, he was constantly surrounded by people; the deference to him was mind-boggling. Su-

san watched as the groupies appeared as if from nowhere, trying every trick imaginable to gain his
attention. Despite all the confusion, Bruce demanded
that she be by his side at all times, even going so far as
to send one of his lackeys for her if she was away for
too long a time. Always she and Bruce were formal
and remote with each other, holding conversations at
arm's length with guarded expressions.

With the arrival of each member of the crew and
cast, there seemed to be an acceptance that served to
create friendships. Bruce's female co-star hadn't arrived yet, and one woman Susan found herself talking to more and more was the major makeup artist.
Her name was Ann Gold. She was from London, and
she wore her black hair in one of the biggest frizzed
looks Susan had ever seen. She always had a quick
smile and an eager way about her, and Susan liked her
so much that she would often go by and watch as Ann
worked experimentally on different cast members.

One late afternoon, when Susan was watching her
contour the face of a woman who would be playing the
role of a nurse in the picture, Ann said, "Hey, you're
next. I've been dying to get my hands on you."

"Oh, no," Susan argued. "I'm not the type."

"Type?" Ann held up a powder brush. "I create the
types myself. Sit down here and let me have a go at
you." She spun the makeup chair around.

Cheeks flushed with embarrassment, Susan accommodated her friend by sitting down where she'd been
instructed, and waiting patiently while Ann covered
her shoulders with a protective cloth and set about

creating a different Susan. It took longer than Susan had thought, what with the experimentation and the hair styling. But when she was finished, Susan tilted her head toward the big mirror in front of her and drew in her breath when she saw herself.

"I don't believe it!" she exclaimed.

"Believe it, kid. You have marvelous cheekbones."

With the contouring makeup, Ann had sculpted shadows on Susan's face, which gave her a look of hollowed-out cheeks of perfect proportions. She'd lined her eyes with kohl crayon and used gold and turquoise eye shadow, which had somehow made Susan's eyes look movie-star size. Her lips were outlined in brightest red and with her hair pulled chicly back and clipped with ornate combs, she looked like a different person.

"I—I don't know what to say. I love it." Susan wasn't sure yet how long she'd love it, but the uniqueness of having this different face staring back at her in the mirror was thrilling.

"You can do it yourself. I'll show you how," Ann was saying when Bruce happened by with another crew member.

He stopped in his tracks before a frown creased his forehead. "Susan?" he asked in a voice that was tentative.

"Yes." She couldn't help but laugh. He hardly recognized her.

"Well, what do you think?" Ann asked him.

He nodded, then shifted his feet, making ready to leave. "It's interesting."

"We could put her in front of a camera right now, don't you agree?" Ann twirled Susan's chair around and around. She was proud of this look she had created.

Abruptly, he took two steps toward them before putting his hand out to stop the chair. His response was made with care this time as he studied Susan's face. "She doesn't need it," he replied.

"No, of course not, but..." Ann's voice faded to silence as the two women watched him stalk away.

When he was out of sight, Susan said, "Thanks, Ann, I appreciate what you've done. I'll leave this on when we go to dinner tonight."

"Yeah, sure." Ann started cleaning up her makeup table. "What do you think was wrong with him? He's never acted like that before, and I've been on two pictures with him." With her hands full of face brushes to be replaced in her case, Ann glanced back in the direction he'd gone. "That's funny, the way he said that."

Susan followed her glance, feeling as if something inside her was twisted. "Maybe it's the altitude," she said reflectively.

The next day she was sitting at a makeshift table with her typewriter in front of her, working with the assistant director on a line of a dialogue that they'd decided might be improved. Right after breakfast that morning, the crew had been driven to the three-story building that would be used as a sanatorium, and she had set up to work under a shade tree away from the others, where she could enjoy the cool Santa Fe air.

On and off she had seen Bruce as he gave the crew directions for what he wanted done, but they had not spoken since the day before. Now she saw him walking toward her table.

A jerk of Bruce's head dismissed his assistant and he took the chair the man vacated. "It has occurred to me that I was rude yesterday when I saw you in the makeup chair," he said.

Susan laid aside her script and took her glasses off, placing them on top of the manuscript with particular care. "I took it that you were being your usual affable self. That's the only way I've seen you lately."

He gave her a sunny smile, but she felt that behind the turned-up mouth he was mocking her. "I can understand your thinking that."

Her eyes swept over him. She sat there waiting, her fingers idly running along the frame of her glasses.

"I thought I'd try to explain myself."

"It's not necessary."

"I want to."

With a shrug of her shoulders, she nodded. "Very well."

"One of the things I liked about you when we first met was that you weren't trying to look like a Hollywood starlet. You were content to be yourself."

"Sitting in Ann's chair didn't change me. It temporarily changed the way I look. That's all."

"Right." He went on. "It goes along with what I told you before, though. You have to be very careful when you get around this artificial environment. I'm a perfect example. I've been created for fan magazines and gossip columns."

"All I did was let Ann apply makeup," she said a trifle defensively.

"What I'm trying to do is explain why I got so angry that night." His voice had grown quieter, and he had moved his hand so that it was a fingertip away from her own.

"I think it's best that we forget all about that night."

"Have you forgotten?" His finger was touching the pulse point of her wrist by the time he'd finished speaking.

She pulled away from him, grabbing her glasses and then accidentally dropping them. "Bruce, it makes me uncomfortable to discuss this with you now. I'm trying to focus strictly on *Temptress*."

"You're not going to answer me, are you?"

She reached down to the ground to retrieve her glasses, feeling as if the cool breeze had turned to oven level heat.

"Mr. Powers," his assistant called from the steps of the sanatorium set. "We need you over here, please."

Bruce stood and looked down at her, but she refused to respond to him. He walked away, glancing back now and then, but Susan had gone back to working on her script.

By the end of the week Julian had them settled in to a rented house located up in the hills overlooking the city. Expensively furnished with the latest conveniences, the stucco house had a balcony that stretched invitingly along the entire back wall, and four enormous bedrooms. There was an Indian fireplace in the living area and all of the furniture had been handmade in Taos. Susan was the first to move in. The hotel had gotten the best of her after a few days, and she settled in to a bedroom that was on the bottom floor as far away from the master bedroom as she could arrange.

Late on her first evening there, Susan had gone out to enjoy the view. Bruce and the others hadn't yet arrived. She was grateful for the time to be by herself. It seemed her first chance in a long time.

She didn't know how long she'd been standing there enjoying the pastel sunset, but she heard the front door slam shut and then his voice over her shoulder. No other man had a voice like his, thundering and seductive at the same time.

"I want to ask you a question, Susan." He started toward her and she turned to look at him, but his face was shadowed by the night.

"Good evening and how are you?" She mocked his rudeness before she spun back away, feeling her heart pounding inside her chest.

"I've got a question for you."

He stood directly behind her, and she could feel his breath as he spoke. It danced and spun close to her ear. She didn't understand the way her body was suddenly taking over for her, alerting her system to a watchful wakefulness.

"What's your question?" She tried to answer with a casual air that would match his week's indifference.

"You know what it is." He grabbed her shoulders and whirled her around to face him.

"No, I don't."

"Would you help me? You heard me in rehearsal today. I can't get it yet."

She had heard him and felt he wasn't as good as he could have been, but she knew it would take time. How could he expect himself to be able to master a complex role in a matter of a few minutes? "It's a complicated role."

"Maybe too complicated."

There was frustration in his voice and a hint of pain. She felt herself begin to respond. "It won't be too complicated for you. I know you can handle it."

Her words were intended to be gentle. He'd spent too much time as a star who was told what he wanted to hear. Now he wanted only the truth.

"There aren't many stars who'd take this on," he assured her. "They wouldn't risk what I'm risking."

"Which is?"

"The possibility of falling on my face, of overnight becoming the laughingstock of Hollywood and America."

"Bruce." Her voice quavered. She raised her hand and then lowered it. How could she reach him? This time when she spoke her voice was even more gentle than before. "You're not going to fail. You're going to have to delve into yourself and pull out emotions you've never had to show before. At least, that's what I think will happen.''

He reached out, wanting to draw her into his arms, and then when he saw her eyes widen in surprise, he abruptly turned away. ''Unless you've been an actor, you can't imagine how hard it is.''

''I'm not an actor, but I think I can understand it a little. Writers do the same thing—digging down into their heart, their soul, baring a little more of themselves each time they try to do a better, more complete job of telling how someone feels.''

His hands gripped her shoulders, tensely at first, then with more care. ''I need your help.''

She looked up into his eyes and saw much more than she'd ever expected. It was a little like looking into his soul, and she tried to look away. But his eyes held her, speaking to her of his need and despite her wishes, his eyes communicated the desire that kept him coming back over and over again to her.

''I'll help you, Bruce,'' she said softly. ''I will.''

His hands shook as he gave her one last longing look. ''Tomorrow,'' he said, and abruptly let go of her as if she were a raging fire he'd been burned by before hurrying from the terrace and out the front door.

Chapter Seven

He'd wanted to sweep her into his arms, but instead he'd walked away, shaking from the emotion-filled encounter, tormented by the desire he hadn't been able to rid himself of, no matter what he'd tried. He'd come close to kissing her, but he knew that wouldn't have been the end of it.

He was tormenting himself. He wasn't stupid. He knew it was a perverse thing he was doing to himself. Insisting on having her near him at all times as they planned for the upcoming filming, manipulating the situation so that she felt forced to stay in the house he'd rented—all of it planned so that he could see her, be near her.

The first time they'd met, he'd convinced himself he wanted her to help him with this film, nothing more. On their second encounter, he'd tried to feel the same emotions, but the time for fooling himself was past now. If he was going to try to pull himself out of the role of the pampered, pawed-over movie star, his first step was going to have to be truthfulness.

The truth was that he found her more enchanting than any woman he'd met before. In comparison to the women he knew in Hollywood, she was far superior. The women who came to Tinseltown, no matter how fresh and naive, soon took on a hardness that resembled the shell of an egg—smooth to look at but hard to the touch. This woman wasn't like that. Instead, she had a lovely calm presence about her, as a creature able to handle whatever happened with grace and charm.

He'd watched her when she'd been rushed into his private plane. He'd seen the shock on her face when he had insisted that she be housed in Santa Fe in the same place as he, and every single time, no matter what she encountered, it seemed that she always recovered with style and a sense of grace that left him full of admiration.

He wanted her. Oh, how he wanted her, but he wanted something more, and he was afraid he didn't know how to go about getting it from her. Being with Susan McCarthy would mean having a relationship, making a commitment. It had been so long since he'd thought about caring that much that he didn't quite know how to go about it. With a woman like Susan, one mistake and he'd be out.

He walked the deserted streets of Santa Fe, talking to himself, and ended up spending the night back at the La Fonda, his mind absorbed with thinking of her instead of the script he wanted so desperately to master. He felt he was a man suddenly faced with more problems than he'd ever imagined. How he was going to succeed with her was on his mind even as he slept.

Early the next morning, before the sun had completely broken over the horizon, he knocked on the door of the rented house. "Susan, it's Bruce. May I come in?"

He could hear her as she went about unlocking the bolt. He could imagine how her slender fingers would touch the hard metal as she worked methodically at opening the door, and he wondered what she'd look like so early in the morning.

"Bruce?" she said and then she let him in, still blinking against the early morning light.

He wanted to tell her how wonderfully natural she looked standing in the doorway with the first rays of morning sun glancing off her, making her tousled hair look as if it were full of golden shots of metallic threads, and softening the edges of her mouth into delicate tenderness. Instead he lowered his eyes and stepped inside the house.

"I brought fresh-roasted hot coffee and pastries they call butterflies, they're so light."

She pulled her cotton robe up around her and crossed her arms. She closed the door and turned to face him. "Are they from La Fonda?"

"Yes." He walked to the dining room and opened his sack, pulling out paper cups and pastries wrapped in waxed paper squares.

"Are you here to work?" Susan looked out the window and then toward the far kitchen wall, trying to see the clock.

He grinned. "I thought we might as well."

"At ten minutes after six on a Sunday morning?" she asked incredulously, adding a few extra syllables to the word 'morning' with a lilting drawl.

"No time like the present."

She stared at him for a moment, admiring that little-boy grin of his, but she could see the seriousness in his eyes.

"Whew," she said with a sigh. "I think I may have gotten more than I bargained for. Last night I could tell that you wanted this a great deal, but your enthusiasm is a little overwhelming."

He was still grinning. "You haven't seen anything yet," he said, and his eyes settled on her, making Susan instantly aware of that smoky look of his, the one that proclaimed him the owner of some enormously satisfying secret.

Unable to resist his appeal, she smiled back at him. "Give me a minute or two to get dressed and brush my teeth." Grabbing the coffee and still clutching her robe tightly around her, she went into her bedroom and shut the door.

The toothpaste tasted of mint and she swirled the brush across her teeth, staring at the reflection of herself in the bathroom mirror. She was wide awake now. All her senses were alert.

Her recovery had not been as swift as she would have liked, but she hoped she'd done a decent job of concealing her misunderstanding. Now she was prepared. She knew once and for all what it was that he wanted from her, and she was prepared to give it to him, although which of them would deserve the Oscar for the performance when it was all said and done, she wasn't yet sure.

All she knew was that she'd let herself want this man, want to be with him, and it had been a foolish thing to do. She'd have to be strong to take on the commitment she'd made to help him. At the same time she'd have to be strong enough to resist her own needs.

She threw on a pair of jeans and her new blue silk blouse, brushed her hair behind her ears and dabbed her lips with coral lipstick. There wasn't time for anything else, she thought, and besides, it made no difference. He wasn't interested in the womanly part of her. He was intent on mastering the script. For the good of both of them, Susan vowed to swallow her pride and help him do it.

When she came back upstairs she was carrying her reading glasses and a pair of tan huaraches. She sat down on the white linen sofa and, jamming one of the earpieces to her glasses into her mouth, bent over to slip her sandals on. "Okay," she mumbled with the glasses clenched between her teeth, "what first?"

He watched her, absorbed by the way she moved. She was the most natural woman he'd ever met. She wore no makeup; she looked as though she'd hardly bothered brushing her hair. Most women he'd known spent more time in front of the makeup mirror than anyplace else, and yet here she was, as intriguing as anyone he'd ever seen, her very naturalness making the pink blush in her cheeks, the clearness in her eyes, the fine nose a vision of loveliness. He couldn't take his eyes off her.

"I said, what first?" she repeated.

He cleared his throat. "Why not begin at the beginning?" He was trying to push all thought of her away, but it was one of the hardest things he'd done in a long time.

"Okay." She put on her glasses and reached for her script, which was lying on the coffee table. "Page one." She looked up at him, her eyes enormous-looking through her rounded lenses. She gave a short laugh. "You know, I really don't know what I'm doing. I've never done this before." She leaned back on the sofa. "You tell me what we should do."

He looked at her then, interested in the way she was so casually sure of herself, even when she wasn't sure of what she was doing. The admiration he felt for the strength he saw in her filled him with an ache that he found indescribable. He shook his head, more to shake away the power of his sudden swell of emotion than anything else.

When she was putting the first bite of pastry into her mouth, Bruce said, "I know it's crazy of me to be so anxious, but I think you can help me."

She took a bite before speaking. "I want to help you, Bruce."

"I appreciate it. I just want you to know from the start that I appreciate your help."

For the first time, their eyes met. Susan realized as she stared into the blue-black depths of his that the house had grown silent. With no one else there but the two of them, she felt a twinge of uneasiness, particularly since her heart had started such an erratic pounding.

"This is going to be a great movie," she told him, and when he gave her an agreeing nod, it was as if they were making a silent commitment between themselves. They would work well together.

"I'm rushing you. You haven't even had a chance to eat your pastry and I'm trying to get you to start work." He put out his hand to her. "Come on outside. Grab your coffee and your butterfly. We'll watch the sun come up."

They went out on the balcony and sat down. The sky was filled with streaks of palest orange and gold. The top of the sun was peeping over the horizon. They didn't speak until they'd finished drinking their coffee.

Bruce saw her shiver once. The morning air was still chilly. "Let's go back in."

He put his arm around her shoulders to warm her and walked back inside with her. "How about my starting a fire—a little one that will just take the coolness off the morning air?''

"I'd love it," she answered, feeling at once confused and lost. His act of placing his arm around her had been an intimacy she didn't feel at all comfortable with.

She had promised to help him. She'd given her word. There was no turning back. But she'd forgotten her own needs and desires when she'd said yes. She'd momentarily chosen to ignore the reactions he created inside her. How, she wondered, when the energy between them seemed sometimes so powerful it might explode.

Susan shook her head as she watched him work with the fire. Talking to herself about an irreversible mistake would do no good. She'd just have to hold tight to her emotions, keep them in check somehow.

The piñon wood sparked with fire in only a few seconds as everything had been set out sometime before inside the Indian fireplace. Bruce had only to light the fire starter and watch it catch. "This won't take a minute," he told her, but when he looked back over his shoulder he saw her staring out the window. She seemed not to have heard him.

He was enjoying having no one else around to interfere with them. He felt comfortable with Susan, and he supposed that was why he felt that with only her in the house he still had privacy. He wanted no distractions when they were alone. "There it goes."

"I love to smell the piñon wood." She stood and walked over to his side. "Now I'll take a second cup of coffee," she told him, as she made her way into the kitchen. "Then I'll be ready to get to work."

Through the passageway, he watched her refill her cup. "Good. I'm ready, too. I want to start with the scene where he confesses to his wife that he can't control the cocaine."

"No," she said quickly. "I'd rather not. I think we should start with the scene where he's in the police station and the doctor stops by to talk to him."

The scene between Lanny and his wife was too emotional. Susan knew she wasn't ready for it, no matter what Bruce's opinion was. The scene built up to the two of them falling into each other's arms, desperate to try to breach the gap that had developed between them. It was definitely not anything she wanted to try with Bruce. She'd have to build up to it when she was feeling stronger. Maybe after she saw how their rehearsals went she'd be more at ease, better prepared. For now she remained wary. There was too much chemistry between them right now.

Bruce stared at her for a moment. Then he shrugged and, picking up his manuscript, began turning back the pages from the one he had previously marked. "Okay. Whatever you say." His voice sounded as if he was curious, but he didn't say anything more.

They sat on the linen sofa, as far as possible from each other. Susan drank her coffee and watched the crackling fire.

He watched her for a slow second. Then he said, "This Lanny." He pointed to the script. "How did you ever come to know his kind of pain?"

She tried to smile to let him know that she understood his asking. "I have . . . had a friend. He was my Lanny."

"He's dead?"

Susan nodded, then looked away. She let her eyes trace the line of hills in the far distance through the living room window.

The silence between them grew. An ember popped in the fireplace. They both turned their heads to see if the ember had flown out of the fire and onto the Navajo rug arranged between the sofa and the fireplace. There eyes met.

"Tell me about your Lanny," Bruce urged gently.

She didn't want to; it was too personal. But she wanted this movie to be better than average. She had to help give it every advantage she could.

"Very well," she said. There was some residual hesitation in her voice, but she pushed on. "The man was a dear friend of mine. He and I had known each other since we were four years old and went to our first session of Sunday school at the First Baptist Church."

Piece by piece she told her story—how they'd both dreamed of going to Hollywood, Susan as a screenwriter, her friend as a cinematographer. He'd made it before Susan.

Through some of his disturbing middle-of-the-night calls and the more timely but no less frantic ones from his young California wife, Susan was able to figure out what was happening to him. It was a case of too much too soon. Fast success, fast money and fast ways of pleasuring himself. Cocaine was the habit of the eighties, and it was steadily available both at work and at play. Susan had observed his avoidance, his paranoia and his denial with a sad heart, until one day she'd received word of his death.

"So you see..." There were tears stinging her eyes. "This story is a tribute to Lanny. It's the way his story could have, should have, gone."

Bruce reached across to her, his hand outstretched in a gesture of friendship and caring. Without thinking, she allowed herself to turn so that her hand could join his. They sat that way for a moment.

"Well," he sighed. "Let's see if we can do your Lanny justice. What do you say?"

Susan nodded, appreciating this man who seemed so willing to show the compassionate side of himself. "Let's go."

"Page thirteen. Lanny tells..."

That day they rehearsed for six hours straight. By evening Johnny Day had brought over his boss's things from the hotel and the cook had arrived, as well as Bruce's secretary, who had been shown her room. A hundred details had been taken care of. But the two of them had not been bothered. Bruce had seen to that.

The next day they followed the same schedule. And the next.

"I want to get into your mind," Bruce found himself repeating, and from time to time he realized that he had not meant his comments for the script alone. He was enjoying her immensely. She made him feel good. As she walked him through the script, she was sharing her confidence with him; it was a remarkable feeling.

By week's end the crew was good-naturedly teasing Susan, calling her the director's assistant. Ted Willis, who actually had the job as assistant director, didn't seem to mind her working closely with Bruce. "That's good," Ted told her one evening when they were all gathered for dinner in an out-of-the-way restaurant off the square. "Bruce uses you to help him think the actor's scenes through. I get left the hard part, making sure the scenes are perfect for all the shots." He'd winked at her. "See, Susan, this way I get to sort of be my own boss, and learn from Bruce at the same time."

Susan was feeling an overwhelming sense of pride. Slowly but surely Bruce was becoming more confident in himself and his role as Lanny. He wasn't without his weak spots still, but he was letting himself go, opening himself up more and more to the pain and agony of the script.

During the following week, they sandwiched their rehearsals into the actual shooting schedule. "I want to rehearse that scene between Lanny and his wife tonight," Bruce whispered into her ear just before he stepped into the harsh lights of the cameras and said "Action."

Susan watched him as he acted the scene with the sanatorium doctor. As she watched the scene build, she thought back over the times they'd been together. Each day it was getting harder and harder for her to keep him at arm's length. They'd started out working together for a common goal. Then they'd become friends. Now she was aware more than at any other time in the past of the attraction between them, the blinding appeal that drew them together. Everything they did, anything they did, only served to make it worse.

" 'There's nothing wrong with me,' " Bruce was saying in his role as Lanny. He stared defiantly at the doctor, and all the crew was silent, watching his performance.

" 'Is that why you're about to lose your wife and your daughter? Is that why you can't go two hours without a snort?' " The actor playing the doctor's role used his voice well as he challenged the sick man before him.

The cameras moved in for a close-up, and Susan watched intently. A tear started at the corner of Bruce's left eye and began to roll slowly down his cheek. The camera had panned to his face, carefully following the progress of the tear. Then Bruce began to cry, great gasping sobs that sounded as if his body was racked with each cry.

Despite herself Susan felt a wave of sympathy rush through her, and then the tears began. One by one, they fell against the knuckles of her hands as she futilely tried to wipe them away. When Bruce was finished with the scene, there wasn't a dry eye in the group, and the lights were turned off after his assistant yelled "Cut" over the sound of clapping of hands that roared all around them.

"How was it?" Bruce asked when they were on their way back to the rented house.

"Don't tell me you don't know." She couldn't believe her ears. "You were magnificent."

"It's hard, Susan." He looked at her, his eyes full of doubt. "You can't know how hard this is for me."

Instinctively, she reached out and brushed his hand with hers. "You're doing a great job. Believe that."

He looked away, deciding to say no more about it. He was shaky, but as long as he had her by his side, she gave him a certain edge of strength he needed. She seemed so sure of him that it made him feel more sure of himself, even though he still had many doubts about this role. It was too difficult for simple explanations.

"How about having Maria fix up bowls of chili or something easy like that with a good red wine? Then we'll rehearse that other scene—the one between Lanny and his wife. The scene is bugging me."

"Sure," she replied, although she wasn't feeling any too sure. The scene was an intimate one, very intimate.

"I've told Johnny I didn't want anybody around tonight till midnight. I don't want any interruptions," he announced, wondering if he shouldn't move everyone else out except for Susan and Johnny. He glanced at her. No, he thought. Better not try it. She wouldn't like that idea one bit.

From the beginning, the cook named Maria had been completely won over by Bruce. She met them at the door, her rotund body and her single long black braid shaking as she talked. "I been waiting to see what you want to eat." Maria had eyes only for Bruce.

"You're wonderful," Bruce told her, patting her shoulder as he stepped inside. "Blue corn tortillas and a bowl of chili."

"Maybe with my cooking you're going to get fat, Mr. Powers, and then nobody will come to see you in the movies." She followed him into the living room and Susan trailed behind them, enjoying the fun they were having.

"Yeah, but I'm not worried, Maria. You'll still come and bring all your family. That's a good twenty or so tickets."

"Ha," the round woman laughed. "Maybe you give them to me free."

"For a bowl of hot chili and blue corn tortillas, I'll give you as many tickets as you want." He looked back at Susan. "I'm going to take a quick shower."

"Me too."

"And you, miss, you want the same to eat?" Maria asked Susan.

"Yes, please."

"Be back here in forty-five minutes. I will have the chili hot." Maria looked at Bruce.

"We'll be back." Bruce gave them both an elaborate wink, then headed to his bedroom while Susan went downstairs to hers. They'd have to hurry to make Maria's deadline. She wouldn't tolerate anyone being late, not even Bruce.

After supper, Maria cleaned the kitchen and left them alone. As a concession to the cool evenings of

Santa Fe, Bruce lit a fire and they finished off the last of their wine.

Susan was exhausted. It seemed they'd been going nonstop for over two weeks. After a hot shower and a warm meal, she felt like relaxing. She leaned back against the sofa and let her eyes shut out the world.

"You look so pretty sitting there, I hate to bother you," he said from the other side of the sofa.

"But..."

"But are you ready to rehearse?"

She opened her eyes and sat up. There was a smile of agreement on her face. "Sure. Anytime you are."

"First, I have something for you." He walked back in the direction of his bedroom and reappeared with a gift-wrapped package.

"What's this?" she asked when he thrust it into her hand.

"Just a little thank-you. It's not enough, but hopefully it's a start."

Bruce grinned at her. She looked up in time to catch sight of a flash of shining blue-black eyes, white, white teeth and generous lips.

Opening the present, Susan felt all thumbs. "I'm tearing the ribbon. I can't wait for the scissors."

He laughed. "At least I've made a hit in one way. It's obvious to me that you like surprises."

Smiling, she tore the wrapping paper. "As a kid, I never got enough. I can't help myself. It's a permanent condition now."

"I'd like to do something about it."

His declaration made her head shoot up. She stared. What did he mean by that, she wondered. But he gave away nothing. He only smiled.

"Looks like you already are," she finally answered, taking more time to open the heavy white box. "Oh, Bruce, you shouldn't have," she exclaimed, lifting up a heavy antique silver belt with chunks of turquoise embedded in the center of each silver piece. "Oh, my." She stood up and wrapped the belt around her waist. She thought it was the most wonderful piece of jewelry she'd ever seen. A practical work of art.

"It's very old," he said.

"I love it." She went to look at her reflection in the window near the fireplace.

"It looks great on you."

"This—" She paused to look down at the belt. "This must have... I can't accept this, Bruce. It's worth far too much money."

"I won't let you give it back to me." He studied her. "You need to wear it often. They say it will bring good luck to the wearer."

"I can't wait," she said, deciding that she couldn't ruin his surprise by refusing it.

"Good. I like a woman who doesn't act coy when a man wants to bestow gifts on her." He took a step toward her, but thought he saw a warning glint in her eye. "Well," he said, taking up his wineglass and draining it. "Wear your belt while we rehearse."

He thought she looked much too inviting with the ancient belt slung down over her faded jeans. She wore a plain white silk blouse and her curly hair flew around her face without restraint. Susan wore no makeup. Her face was gleaming with good health, just the way he liked to see her.

"Yes, I will." She walked around the room and then went back to look at her reflection. "It's really a stunning belt." Slowly, she turned to Bruce. "Thank you," she whispered.

"You're very welcome." This time he resisted the urge to take a step toward her, although he found it almost impossible.

With her hand on the belt, Susan went back to sit on the sofa. "Now I'll have to really work hard helping you, won't I?"

"You already are."

Lit by the flames from the fire, Bruce's eyes were shining when she looked over at him. Susan thought he'd never seemed more provocative, with his shoulders slung back so that his arms were braced along the back of the sofa, his hips thrust forward and one leg bent across the other. He had a satisfied look about him. He seemed completely relaxed. It was an inviting look.

They began working on the scene. Bruce read his lines from the script at first, but gradually he stopped looking at it. He'd memorized his lines.

"'Honey, things will be better. I promise.'" Bruce spoke the lines perfectly, using just the right intonation of a man trying to rebuild his hope.

"'I don't know, Lanny. There have been too many promises made and broken.'" Susan recited the lines of the role of Lanny's wife.

"'I know.'" Bruce nodded. His face was filled with pain. "'But I need you. I can't do this without you.'"

"'You're the only one who can do it, Lanny.'"

"'But I can't do it alone,'" he cried. "'I have to know that you're behind me.'"

"'What are you asking from me? What is it that you want?'"

He paused for effect. "'Do I have to say it?'"

She didn't answer, letting the emotion build.

"'I want to hear you say you love me. I want to know that you still desire me.'"

His eyes washed over Susan, with her seductive, enticing eyes. "'I do.'" Her answer was accompanied by a choking feeling. It was one thing to write a script. It was quite another to act it with a man like Bruce.

"'Say it,'" he whispered. His request was full of agony and longing just like Lanny's would be.

"'I love you, Lanny.'"

"'And?'"

"'And I want you. I've never stopped wanting you.'"

With one sure move, Bruce was across the sofa. He was mere inches away from her, his eyes staring into hers.

"'Prove it,'" he taunted.

Susan knew the lines so well, had written them to be portrayed with just this much drama, but hearing Bruce speak them and feeling the stirrings of hunger that were invading her every breath, Susan faltered. "'I...'" She couldn't think of the next line.

"I think we should just drop her next line and go on to the embrace," Bruce declared in his huskiest voice. "There's no need for her to say anything more. It only detracts from the importance of the emotional upheaval they're going through." He brushed his lips across her cheek and across to the shell of her ear.

"That's enough," she said in protest, raising her arms to shield her body from his. But her defense was lackluster at best.

When his lips found hers, the pressure was enough to still any sort of protest she might have left. She was left with a web of excitement weaving its spell through her as his mouth sent seductive messages of their very own.

The intrusion of Bruce's tongue into the warmth of her open mouth proved to be a welcome one, and she allowed herself the pleasure of responding to him. The hands that had gone to his chest in protest now moved up along his neck to welcome him.

They positioned their bodies against each other so that they were locked in an embrace that had them clinging together. Susan liked the way her body felt against his. She liked the fiery feel of having her breasts respond to the hard masculine chest and the heat that emanated between them.

He pulled back and drew in a deep breath. His eyes met hers as gently, ever so gently, he wove his fingers slowly through her hair.

Susan was trembling. She wanted to say something. She knew she should. How many times had she thought about the repercussions of allowing his touch to enflame her again?

But he took the chance away from her as he bent again to take her lips with his. A moan of pleasure escaped him as he plunged his tongue inside her warmth and hers met his. With one hand still running through her silky hair, his other escaped to edge down her spine, caress her hip and then stop momentarily along the length of her thigh.

Everything he did was perfection at its peak. Every move he made left her wanting more. Every stroke of his tongue made her thrill to its touch. This was an experience she hadn't known before, this sudden rippling of desire, this mindless abandon. No other man had ever awakened the white-hot passion she was feeling.

Susan explored his face with her fingers, stopping once to let herself memorize by touch the cleft in his chin, which she'd come to admire. The cleft that kept his looks from being too handsome, too magnificent—she adored his imperfection, slight though it was.

All the time that she was running her fingers over the angles and planes of his face, she was responding to the kneading movements he was making with his hand against her thigh. Hearing him moan with desire had left her feeling hot and wanting.

Suddenly, as he was about to make a move so that they could lie together across the sofa, the thought struck Bruce that this was no ordinary woman he was holding in his arms. She meant more to him than any conquest.

He pulled away, slowly nuzzling her neck with his warm lips, allowing his hand to trace a heated path back along her hip and across her breast. Now that they knew where this rehearsal would lead, he would wait until they could both agree on what was to happen between them. With this precious woman he wanted no mistakes to be made. If he tried to make love to her now, she might see it as their yielding to the heat of the moment. Bruce wanted more. He wanted her to come willingly, without a script.

"This rehearsal is going to have been much better than the actual shot," he told her. "I'll ask you tomorrow if you'll rehearse this scene with me one more time."

"Why tomorrow?" she asked, confused by the sudden change in him.

"It will be better that way." His eyes held hers, studying her reaction. "Believe me," he said softly. "Tomorrow I intend to act out the scene in its entirety."

"Oh," Susan gasped, taking in the full impact of his words.

"I'll ask you again then. Now it's time for us to call it a night."

Susan went to bed, still reeling from the fire of his touch, stung by the implications of his speech. She didn't know what to think or even if she could think at that point.

Chapter Eight

All night long, Susan's mind went in a thousand different directions, as had happened with far too much frequency since she'd met Bruce Powers. It was hard on her physically, as well as emotionally.

Her face felt flushed when she thought about how easily she'd melted into Bruce's inviting arms. It disturbed her that she'd shunted aside all the fears and concerns she'd had about him before. Instead she'd let her heart and her body respond to his touch.

Where were all the doubts she'd had about him? That he would try to repay her kindness with the only sure way he knew of doing so—by inviting her to share an embrace with the Dream Lover. Gossip said it was a common enough happening in Hollywood. Then he would drop her after—after what, she wondered, stopping herself in the middle of her thoughts.

How was it that she had subconsciously planned ahead for this? When was it that she'd already visualized herself as the one left abandoned and disillusioned?

Oh, Susan, she said to herself. *Be honest. At least be honest about what you feel for Bruce Powers. Let it out.*

She tossed and turned in the bed, then finally sat up and watched the morning sun rise on the horizon, a bright orange ball of flame.

What she felt for Bruce was a longing that would not go away. Even though she was afraid that she'd end up hurt, she wanted him. She was afraid of Hollywood, afraid of the life that it inspired, but she was also afraid she could not deny Bruce if he were to come to her again. And he would come. After what he'd said last night, she had no doubt about that.

Morning brought little relief except distraction. As soon as she was dressed and upstairs, Susan was caught up in the daily projects that were part of making a movie. She ate a quick breakfast and met with Bruce's co-star to discuss a change in her lines. Over coffee, she talked to the assistant director, who told her Bruce had left early in the morning to go out to the sanatorium location. He'd wanted to check out the lighting in the morning hours.

She didn't see Bruce until lunchtime. He entered the house with three people following him. He seemed always to be busy, and Susan marveled at how he could keep it all together.

"Hello, there," he said with a quick wink.

Before she could answer, his attention was drawn away by the people who were waiting to see him. She waited patiently while he soothed his co-star's anxiety, told his assistant when they would schedule the next sanatorium scenes, answered Maria's inquiries about dinner and then answered a half dozen more questions before he could turn to her again.

"Susan," he said loudly, glad to have so many people around him. "I'd like to rehearse that scene one more time tonight. All of it this time." He watched her, not at all sure how she would react but nevertheless hopeful.

Her flesh prickled with anticipation. She couldn't believe he was doing this. Yet he'd warned her, hadn't he?

In the cold light of day when there were people all around them, she told herself she shouldn't be feeling this way, shouldn't be responding like this. It did little good.

"We'll see," she answered, her eyes staring into his. She hoped her voice hadn't betrayed the emotion she was feeling.

Susan knew she was playing a game of Russian roulette with her heart. She wasn't a woman who wanted to spend a night with the Dream Lover. She was the kind who was full of feelings and needs that had to be answered before she could think of going to bed with a man, particularly a man of Bruce's reputation from a town with its own sordid reputation.

"Good enough" was all that he said. He took his eyes off her but not before she'd seen a trace of a delicate smile around the corners of his mouth.

"Maria," he called. "Tonight there will be two for dinner. Fix us a surprise. Something delightful," he added.

"Yes, sir." There was an instant sound of a pan banging and singing as soon as the cook returned to the kitchen. Maria was already at work.

The rest of the afternoon was much like the morning. Everyone was busy trying to do the assigned tasks. It was just as well, Susan thought. She didn't want to do any more thinking. Every time she did, her insides tightened up as though she were a spring about to come unwound. Yet something inside her was spurring her on. She didn't know if she could stop herself if she wanted to.

By eight o'clock, Bruce had chased everyone out of the house. Maria had a meal of fresh fillet of red snapper, which she had marinated in capers and fresh lime juice. She'd made yeast rolls and a green bean salad that was divine.

"You're going to make me fat, Maria," Bruce remarked when she added to their plates.

"I think it might be true," Maria answered in her lilting voice. "You like Maria's food."

"I sure do."

"I do, too," Susan added, knowing that Maria cared only about Bruce's reaction.

"I can teach you to cook this way," Maria offered, and Susan was surprised at the woman's generosity.

"I'd like that if I have any time while we're here," Susan told her, knowing full well that the offer was being made because of Maria's affection for Bruce.

"We won't." Bruce was heaping more green beans on his plate. "We'll have this wrapped up by the end of the week and then we'll go back to L.A. to finish up."

Susan smiled at him, but she couldn't help but feel a wave of regret at his announcement. She'd enjoyed the beauty of Santa Fe, and most of all she'd enjoyed the time she'd shared with Bruce. L.A. seemed like an intrusion. Here in Santa Fe she didn't have the same kinds of fears and concerns she had had back in Hollywood. Here, she could fantasize that their lives were practically normal.

It was silly of her to think that way, but she couldn't help but feel their going was ill timed right now. She wished they could stay where they were, yet she realized it was a ridiculous wish.

The wish was ridiculous, but Susan was aware of the fact that there were many things she'd engaged in lately that could be classified as ridiculous on her part, particularly her agreeing to work with Bruce tonight when she knew exactly where it would lead. But then again, what could be so wrong about being with a man who had the ability to make her go weak with desire with just the slightest touch of a hand or a brush of his lips across hers?

"Of course we won't go until we get these next four or five scenes worked out," he told her. "They're the most crucial."

She nodded. "I rewrote those two lines we discussed last night."

"Speaking of last night," he told her as he finished off a bit of fish, "I've thought about you all day long. You've interfered with my work, Susan."

"I hope that's not so. The movie's the important thing," she answered, made suddenly shy by his declaration.

"The movie's important. So are we, though." His eyes had locked with hers.

For a long while, she returned his stare. All she could think of was how wonderfully charming, how nice a man he was. They seemed to have gotten along so well in the past weeks and it wasn't just the chemistry, although that was extremely powerful. The thing was that they'd become comfortable companions, friends as well as a man and a woman brought together by fate and kept together by unseen forces.

They didn't speak again as they finished their meal. While they had coffee laced with Amaretto in the living room, Maria cleaned up the kitchen and left them alone in the house.

When Susan heard the woman carefully close the door behind her, she felt momentarily rattled. Maybe she shouldn't stay, either. She hadn't thought this thing through enough. None of her old fears had been resolved, only obscured.

"Susan," he said in a voice that seemed to engulf her with its powerful resonance. He walked to her side. "What's the matter?"

She turned to face him. "Oh, I don't know."

"Let's talk, you and I." He took her hand and led her to the built-in bench that ran along the outside of the fireplace.

Reluctantly, Susan followed him, mindful of her half-full cup of coffee as she did so. She felt full of conflict, wanting what she knew would please her, but afraid that her momentary pleasure could quickly change to pain.

Bruce leaned against the wall near the window, looking out on the starry night sky. There were still faded streaks of orange and pale yellow where the sun had left its trail.

Susan sat near, but apart from him. She looked out through the massive window, staring up at the bright stars as she drank her coffee. She was still feeling apprehensive, and over and over she ran her hand along the soft silk cuffs of her blouse.

"Susan, don't be nervous with me. I don't want you to be." When he spoke he was still looking out at the darkening night.

"I wish I could pick and choose when I wanted to be nervous and when I didn't. I don't, however—" she stopped to laugh "—have that much control."

Bruce smiled with her. "I know what you mean."

"You mean you still get nervous about things? You certainly don't look like you do." She brushed away a strand of curly hair that had fallen across her fore-head.

His eyes cut to her, and then he turned so that he was looking straight at her. "Of course I do. I'm human, too," he told her with a touch of irritation.

She said nothing, but he refused to take his eyes from hers. Finally she stood up, put her coffee cup on a nearby table and came back to sit beside him.

He relaxed his head against the wall and propped his left foot up on the bench. Then he slung his arm across the top of his knee, the picture of a comfortable man.

"One of the things that I liked about you when we first met, besides the fact that you're pretty and smart and your own woman, was that you didn't seem particularly impressed with the star, Bruce Powers. Most people look at the star. They don't seem interested in the man."

She thought of the impression she'd had when she'd first met him. "Maybe you don't let them see the real man, the person behind the star."

He mulled over what she'd said. Then he reached out and took her hand and laid it with his between them on the bench. The action seemed too natural for her to think much about it, except that she liked the gentle touch of his hand and its warmth when it enveloped hers.

"You may be right. I'll have to think about that. I've always thought that it was a problem I had after I became known as a star." His finger began to move slowly back and forth along her hand.

She looked at him. "When I first met you that day in Dirkson's office I thought you were a phony." She tried to temper her truth with an apology. "I know that's not true now."

He grinned. "A phony? Hmm." He repositioned himself on the bench, moving closer to her, yet all the while his hand held hers tightly. "Maybe that's something I developed to fit my image." His grin returned. "Of course, if what you're saying is true, then I'm the one with the problem. I was thinking it was everyone else, you see."

Now it was her turn to smile. "Isn't that what we all do?"

"What?"

"Blame our problems on someone else."

"More or less." He took his hand away and eased his arm around her shoulder. "Hollywood is a difficult place to be yourself. After you reach the top, everybody wants a piece of you."

"I'm sure that's particularly true in your case." She felt the pressure of his arm as he pulled her to him.

She knew that if she let things continue the way they were going, she would be responsible for whatever happened. Without another thought, she yielded and put her head on his shoulder, and both of them turned to face the flame from the fire.

"Yeah. The truth is that my image has nothing to do with me."

"You mean the Dream Lover?" She was smiling as she teased him.

"Yeah. I'm probably not even a good lover. Who knows?"

"I'll bet you don't have many complaints." After she'd said it, she could feel his shoulders as he shrugged his answer.

"Who would know if maybe they don't complain because they're with a star who might be able to do something for them, or if they don't know any better?" he said facetiously. "I sure don't know."

She wanted to laugh at the clever way he had of describing all the possibilities so self-deprecatingly, but she sensed that he wasn't thinking of this conversation as being a funny one at all.

"Well, at least you haven't had any complaints."

"How about you? Have you had any complaints? I won't believe you if you tell me yes." His voice dropped a notch. "How could anyone ever be disappointed in you?"

"Me?" She turned, giving him an incredulous look. She hadn't heard the compliment, only the extremely personal question. She was busily racking her brain for an answer. "Well, I guess not, but then I haven't..." She didn't finish her statement.

"Known as many men as I have women? I guess you read all the Hollywood trash sheets, too, huh?"

"That wasn't what I was going to say." Her voice became tight. "I was going to say that I haven't had much experience. I was always working. I didn't have much time for men in my life." She gave him a quick look. "I wasn't going to say anything about you, Bruce."

"Take it from me, the whole thing's vastly over-rated."

His statement came as a surprise, but this time she kept her expression cool and calm. "What do you mean?"

"I mean that contrary to what you've probably read about me, I don't want different women all the time. I'm looking for one woman. I want somebody who'll love me if I have two flops in a row and my Rolls gets repossessed. I want somebody who'll love me if I'm in a car wreck and my face gets smashed up. I want a woman who'll look beyond the exterior."

"With all the attention you get, I wouldn't think that would be hard at all." She was amazed at his revelation. He seemed so down-to-earth, this movie star who was sharing his innermost secrets with her.

He tightened his hold. "That's just it. Ever since I hit Hollywood, it's been hard. I haven't found a woman who could see through the hype to the real Bruce Powers."

Susan felt a tug on her heart when he spoke. His words were having a tremendous impact.

"Maybe you've been looking in the wrong places," she said softly.

Bruce rose up and reached out to gently grasp her chin. Ever so slowly he turned her face toward him. "You're a very bright young woman," he murmured. "You always seem to have the right answer."

He kissed her lips gently, barely a touch, once, twice before raising both hands to take her face and press his mouth against hers. His kiss began with sweet purpose, but when he felt her arms tentatively wrap around his neck and her body fall ever so slightly against his, his kiss became hungry, more intense.

Suddenly Susan was pressed against the wall as his mouth worked on hers. When her tongue met his, the kiss became liquid fire, and she felt herself wanting to resist when he pulled slowly away.

"You're too tense, Susan. We're going to have to do something about that," he said through lips that would not leave hers but instead hovered there, brushing against her with that same touch of liquid fire. "You need so badly to relax when you're with me." He concentrated all his attentions on her finely shaped lips. He was determined that she would begin to want him as much as he wanted her.

At first he held on to his hunger, allowing his mouth to work along hers with the lightest sweep, settling into the corners, then moving out to withdraw before covering her mouth with his own and pressing his tongue along the swell of her lips. When he could feel the muscles in her body begin to relax, he allowed his tongue to invade her, his entire being centered on pleasing her.

Susan felt Bruce's hands move demandingly over her, and she responded to his touch, all control gone from her, as if it had been burned out with the heat of his kiss. She didn't care what happened, seized as she was by his attentions. There was no future, no past, only her own impulses urging her on. She wanted only to feel this man's magical touch and find an answer to the sharp needs he'd awakened in her.

Bruce warned himself to go carefully with this precious woman. She was unlike any other before her, and so to him she seemed a delicate thing. But his body was demanding to know her, and he was helpless to slow what they both were responding to with their own silent urgings.

"Let's go to my room," he said, breathing hard.

If she had tried to refuse him, Susan didn't know if he would have obeyed her; he seemed so intent on getting them where he thought they should be. With her wrist enclosed in his grasp, he pulled her with him, never taking his eyes from hers as they walked.

When they were inside the bedroom, with one full sweep Bruce pulled the coverlet from the bed and then quickly brought her back into his arms. "I can't wait for you, Susan. I want to see you," he whispered before his lips danced along hers again.

His mouth, covering hers, was sending her messages of demand and his body pressed hard against hers was also telling her of his desire. He deftly stripped off her belt and then her jeans.

Running her fingers through his thick dark hair, Susan was responding as she'd never remembered herself responding before. This was an unbelievable experience. Every nerve, every pore in her body seemed to have some element of life, and she was filled with a feeling of pleasure so powerful that she knew she could not have ever imagined anything so delectable.

Quickly, he unbuttoned his shirt and flung it behind him. Somehow he managed to kiss her even as he stepped out of his clothes. She was reveling in the hot kisses that were raining down on her, and she leaned back to allow his mouth easier access to her throat.

If the room was cold, she did not feel it. Instead she felt as if a thousand sparks of heat were firing off inside her. She knew she felt hot to the touch and so, it seemed, did he. His fingers burned into her as he slid them across her silk blouse, loosening the buttons from top to bottom as he went. When finally she was freed of her bra and her panties, his hot hands roamed demandingly across her body, followed by his lips as he studied everything about her with an eager physical exploration that left them both breathless.

Together they moved onto the bed. When they were settled, Bruce pulled the coverlet over them, then covered her body with his own. He held her there until he could feel her tenseness slowly begin to fade away. He could hear the two of them breathing in unison and he didn't move until he could feel her body once again relax. In the darkness from the coverlet, it was as if he'd blocked out the light and the world, leaving only the two of them alone.

His mouth moved hungrily, tasting, assessing. She felt pliant, willing to allow him to do whatever he would so long as he kept her body in this fine-tuned state of bliss.

Bruce knew she wanted him, but he wanted more than that. He wanted her to lose herself in him, just as he was willing to lose himself in her. He wanted to share an experience that she could not dismiss once she'd left his bed.

After a while, he began to allow his fingers to move up and down her spine, then he began to caress her buttocks with the gentlest of touches, slowly, ever so slowly sending his fingertips into a sweep that ended just inside her thighs. When at last he felt her body begin to advance toward his in unspoken need, he was satisfied that he had broken through the constraints she had erected between them.

Bruce bent to suck fiercely on her dark nipples and at the same time inched his hand down in longing discovery. It was then that Susan arched up toward him in uncontrolled response to the way he was making her feel. She was like putty to his touch, gathering herself tight to seek all that he would give her. Her body felt as if she might shudder completely out of control, so much so that she thought she might scream.

Easing her misery, he slipped his hands beneath her as he entered her and began to move inside her. Then she could hear his teeth grinding as their rhythm became united.

Quickly she began to quiver and it was then that she felt her mind fly up and away from her, leaving her a bundle of emotion. She moved her head from side to side, finding the pleasure almost unbearable. At last she sighed, a sigh that went on and on as her body was responding to wave after wave of exquisite passion, unified with his. She began to shudder in long violent spasms, thrown into a final climax.

She heard him moan once, loud and harsh, and then their rhythm began to slow, each of them unwilling to give up the feeling that had overpowered them. A rapturous feeling.

After a while he lay beside her, his hands quietly moving along each line and curve of her body. It was as if he had to know that nothing had changed and that everything was the same.

Just when she thought she was numb and emotionally exhausted, he began to kiss the base of her throat, moving his lips down until he was burying his face in the softness of her cleavage. Again she felt her body respond to him as he wrapped one leg around hers. It was as if once she'd know how much passion he had aroused in her, she would not be satisfied. Suddenly, she felt hot and wanting—wanting him.

Bruce had made love to many women, but she was a special one. This time he wanted to take his time, take her to the edge so they could share that special state of suspension for as long as possible together. Usually he was like a mechanic, accurate and precise. But with Susan he had no control over his feelings or his responses. She made him realize how special a woman she was, extraordinarily special.

For Susan there was no thought of resistance, not any longer. His hands lingered on her breasts, inciting inside her a tingling heat that was about to erupt. His lips replaced his hands as he searched for greater intimacy.

Grasping his hair between her open fingers, Susan urged his head upward until his lips were hovering over hers. She rose up to meet him, longing to feel his warm breath mingled with hers.

As their bodies touched, they were swept away together in a spiraling flight of passion. This time there was a wild eagerness in their lovemaking that was even more tangible than before. This time they knew what erotic thrills were in store for them.

If Susan gave any thought to the consequences of what she was doing, she hurriedly told herself she'd made her bed and she'd have to lie in it. But then she dismissed the thought, because she wasn't lying in it alone. She had the most glorious company any woman could ask for, and she could face her tomorrows tomorrow.

Chapter Nine

The next two days seemed like heaven on earth. Bruce was working with the most important scenes of the movie, and with Susan's help he was performing magnificently. The two of them were more inseparable than ever, together literally day and night, and in Susan's mind it seemed nothing could be added to make her life any more perfect than it was right now.

On Wednesday, Evan Dirkson called Bruce at the house, saying he wanted to see the rushes of the film. Since Susan had been sitting in the living room when Bruce had answered the phone, she couldn't help overhearing Bruce's side of the conversation.

Bruce was trying to stall Dirkson's visit. "Why not wait until we get back to L.A.? We'll set it all up then," he said.

Dirkson said something and then Bruce replied, "I still think it's a better idea for you to wait." He paused, listening. "Yes, yes, I know you've got eleven million dollars tied up in this thing so far. Believe me, I'm watching the budget every day. I know exactly how much you've invested."

Susan heard Bruce's voice change from mellow to brittle. She could virtually feel the anxiety building in him. It was as if the thought of Dirkson's coming to Santa Fe to see the rushes of the movie was more threatening than Bruce could bear. She thought then that she'd had no idea how much it had taken out of this famous actor to risk tackling this particular film.

"Yes, I'll have someone meet your plane. We'll have it all set up," Bruce said into the receiver. "See you then." He hung up but kept his hand on the telephone as he stared at it, momentarily lost in his own thoughts.

When he finally turned around to look at her, Susan could tell there was a visible difference in his expression. He'd been under a lot of pressure. Everyone needed his attentions in order to proceed with the film, and if that wasn't enough, handling the directorial chores as well as the immense strain of the acting that was required were enough to overburden anyone. So far, though, she'd never seen the strain.

Until now. His eyes were dark and moody looking and there were lines around them that were more noticeable than before. His mouth was tight and drawn, and he said nothing, only looked at her.

"Bruce, are you all right?"

"Sure. Why shouldn't I be?" He dropped the subject, made a hasty excuse about needing to see his assistant director and left the house.

When he was outside in the clear night air, he let out a sigh of relief. He needed to be away from everyone to think right now. He was frightened, more frightened than he'd ever been in his life. On an angry whim, he'd set himself up as director of a film in which he needed to expend all his energies in his acting. He was performing in a role more demanding than he'd ever tried before, and although he'd gotten off to a good start, he was getting cold feet. Dirkson's cynical voice had accentuated his concerns. He wanted to believe that with Susan's help he could do this, but right now he wasn't at all sure that he could make this picture a success.

She waited until after midnight in the semidarkened living room. The fire had long since gone out in the fireplace, and she had nodded off to sleep once or twice. Johnny had come in and gone to bed hours earlier. When she could hold her head up no longer, Susan gave up and went to bed.

She didn't see him much the next day, either, and when she did, he didn't have time to talk. He was huddled in conferences with his staff. Shooting was running behind schedule by the afternoon, and she wondered how Evan Dirkson's planned visit had brought about such dramatic changes in Bruce.

She watched him from time to time in the next two days. "What's troubling you?" she asked when he'd taken time to have lunch with the staff and the two of them were walking together to the dining table.

"Nothing," he answered and then shook his head. "I haven't been very attentive to you, I know. But you've got to understand, Susan, I'm busy right now."

"It's not your attentiveness I'm so worried about," she snapped. "It's the sudden change in you."

"You don't understand."

His words were like a wall shutting her out. She felt defensive and lonely at the same time. "How do you know I'm not capable?"

His assistant called to him then and with a troubled look her way, Bruce said, "I have to talk to him. I'll see you tonight."

She sat at the end of the dining table, trying not to look in Bruce's direction. He had hurt her with his words, but she was trying to understand. He was a man with a great many burdens on his back right now, and he needed compassion, not criticism. There was an expression in his dark eyes that seemed to call for her sympathy. She was trying to give it for as long as her patience would last.

Susan realized that if they hadn't shared those few precious nights together, she might not be so willing to try to appreciate his irritability. But something had happened between the two of them that nothing could erase. He'd made her reach out for him, to want him as she'd never dreamed she would do, and she'd felt no hesitation when they'd finally come together. He'd somehow made it possible for her to feel this way.

But now she felt that the closeness they'd shared for that brief period of time was eluding her more with each passing moment. The spirit that had been such a forceful link between the two of them was not as strong as it had been and she regretted its sudden fading away.

Restlessly, she sought the only comfort she'd ever found effective—her own work. That night she stayed up late, after dusting off the typewriter and asking Johnny to carry it to her bedroom. In the back of her mind, she'd been mulling over a new story line and until three the next morning she worked, putting it down on paper.

Shortly after three that morning, she heard a light tapping at her door. In midsentence she stopped her typing. "Who is it?"

"Bruce. May I come in?" His voice sounded grim.

Dressed in her oldest gown and robe and with no makeup, she went to the door, her reading glasses in her hand. "Bruce, it's three o'clock in the morning!" she exclaimed through the closed door.

"I know what time it is." He paused. "But I know you're not sleeping. I heard you hitting the typewriter keys." The sight of her always made him want to take her into his arms, but he was a troubled man, a man who didn't know where to turn. If she hadn't written this script, if she didn't love it so devotedly, he might think differently right now.

She opened the door, and vanity overcame her when she saw him looking at her. "I look terrible."

"Not to me," he declared. "May I come in?" He didn't wait for her permission, but stepped around her and went inside the bedroom. "I just finished with a marathon meeting that's been going on since—" He glanced down at his gold watch. "Since three-thirty this afternoon." He threw himself down across the bed.

Suddenly made uncomfortable by the overwhelming masculinity of the handsome man stretched across the width of her bed, Susan did not look at him, but she thought she smelled alcohol. Instead, she walked back to her typewriter and began stacking her completed manuscript pages.

"Is there something wrong with the script?" she asked, keeping her voice noncommittal while her heart was pounding so hard in her chest that she didn't know if she could hear him when he answered her. Since lunchtime, she'd had this paranoid feeling that everyone was avoiding her, everyone who'd been meeting with Bruce that morning. It could only be because of the script. She could think of no other reason.

"I don't want to talk about this picture anymore right now, Susan, please." He threw his hands across his forehead and closed his eyes. "Evan's coming tomorrow. Need I say more?"

Yes, you do, she wanted to cry out. *I don't understand anything at all about what's going on, and I feel left out, and I don't know why and . . .* She told herself to take it easy. She was becoming Hollywood paranoid, just like all the neurotic, driven people she'd heard about, and she'd vowed not to let that happen.

She took a deep breath. "I'm working on another idea," she told him, wondering if he cared.

"Come over here and sit down by me." He took his hand away from his forehead and patted a spot on the edge of the bed next to him, his eyes still shut tight.

"I'm afraid Evan won't like the picture," he told Susan when she had done as he'd asked.

"Why?" she asked, sensing the tension in him, wanting to help him ease it. When he'd come into her bedroom, it had suddenly seemed filled with a disquiet that literally charged the air.

"He just won't," Bruce said with agitation.

He began to explain that he had a major scene scheduled the next afternoon after Dirkson arrived in the morning for the showing. He said it couldn't be avoided. The scene was already on schedule and because of the scene's requirements, it could not be rescheduled.

"I still don't understand why you're so upset. Everything's been going along fine."

"It's midfilm jitters. I'd like to think so, anyway."

"But I don't see why you feel Mr. Dirkson won't like it. He'll like anything you do."

"Because it's so out of character for me."

"But, Bruce, you're doing a masterful job."

"You would say that. I think I may be making a fool of myself."

"You're wonderful. Everyone says so."

He had finished off four martinis on an empty stomach and couldn't sleep. He'd come looking for solace, but when he saw Susan, he felt guilty. She wouldn't like what he was thinking of doing with the film, but he didn't know who or what to trust right now.

He rolled over and sat up on the edge of the bed. "Are you sure you're not saying that because it's your movie?"

His words stung. Susan couldn't believe her ears. She swallowed hard and sat up straight. "What did you say?"

Bruce tilted his head in her direction. "I'm thinking out loud, wondering if you're not just trying to protect your interests. Everyone else does it. Why shouldn't you?"

With as much dignity as she could muster, Susan gathered her robe tightly around her shoulders and got up. At the door she spun back around and glared at him. "Sometimes you actors forget that not everyone has the same overinflated ego that you seem to have." She threw open the door. "I'm very tired. Good night, Bruce."

He tried to dismiss her anger with a wave of his arm. "I'm sorry, Susan. It's just that if Dirkson starts to laugh tomorrow morning when he sees this film, I think I might have to..."

She was tired of his treatment of her. It wasn't necessary, she thought, and it hurt too much for her to let it continue.

"I don't want to hear any more tonight, Bruce. I don't want to be your whipping boy every time something goes wrong for you with this film."

A red dragon of mistrust had raised its ugly head. She'd worried before that he might confuse need with desire.

He walked out of the bedroom, brushing up against the door frame when he did so, the alcohol fumes strong enough to blow them both down. "I shouldn't have come—"

"You certainly shouldn't." She slammed the door to punctuate her words, feeling her face flush from chin to forehead.

Resolutely, she turned out the lights and went to bed, willing herself to try to sleep. Tomorrow would come soon enough, and she had the feeling that she was now beginning to pay the price for her passion.

Foolishly, she'd hoped Bruce would have come to take her in his arms and find solace in their lovemaking. If he'd even tried to tell her of his doubts and fears with an open heart that was asking for sympathy, she might have felt differently. Those actions she could understand. Instead it was as if he was intent on making her as miserable as he was.

Well, she told herself, she would not play the part. Pride wouldn't let her.

When Evan arrived at the sanatorium location the next morning, Susan knew that Bruce's stormy disposition hadn't changed. He was unusually silent, watching Dirkson as the producer was introduced to the crew and made his way around the site. The screening was set up in a downtown theater for eleven o'clock, and the scene Bruce had worried about was scheduled for three o'clock.

Promptly at eleven, about twelve people were seated in the silent theater, six rows back. Susan sat with Connie, a combination typist and secretary who was interested in writing scripts of her own.

Bruce sat in the center, with Dirkson on his left. When the theater was darkened and the rushes were shown, although they hadn't been edited in sequence yet, the basic thread of the film was evident. Within minutes Susan was spellbound, watching on the big screen the story she'd so lovingly written.

It was hard to watch it the way it was pieced together. She'd seen only finished movies, and the starts and stops made concentration difficult. All she knew when the clips were finished and the lights came back on was that somewhere in all that film was a dynamite movie. Bruce Powers could be proud of his acting and his directing, as well.

No one spoke as one by one they began filing out. Only Evan and Bruce were left inside the theater. When she was walking out into the street, Susan decided she had to go back in. She had to tell him what she thought about the film.

She turned back and hurried inside toward the two figures still standing there. She wondered how Bruce would react to her compliments.

"I want to know what you think. I'm not sure, Evan. I'm too close to it right now."

"I'm not sure, either," she heard Evan say. "It's a shock, Bruce, my boy, a real shock. I'm not saying it's not a good film. I'm saying it's going to surprise your fans. They're going to be sitting on the edge of their seats wondering when you're going to crack one of those crazy jokes of yours."

"And I'm wondering what they'll say when I don't deliver."

"Well, you could always throw in a few zingers every now and then, make it a little lighter, anyway. At the same time you'd be pleasing your loyal fans."

Bruce nodded, and Dirkson patted him on the back. Susan felt like a willful eavesdropper, but she couldn't back away now.

"We'll see," Bruce answered.

"We can always doctor it up a little back in L.A. if we need to." Dirkson patted him again. "I have to admit I'm surprised at you, Bruce."

Susan couldn't tell from his voice whether the surprise had been a good one or not.

"I surprised myself." He couldn't help but feel disappointed. He'd wanted, needed, Evan to rave over the picture and most of all his performance. Evan's lack of conviction made things worse, because one thing about Evan was that he had always been able to spot a winner in the past.

"Well, the way it's written right now, it will either go one way or the other. There won't be any middle ground."

"A bust or a hit."

"Something like that."

"Which way do you predict it will go?" Bruce pushed.

Dirkson shook his head. "I'm not saying just yet. One thing about it, though—you can always choose the middle ground and add those zingers I was talking about." He started to laugh. "Of course, I'd be willing to bet our little screenwriter wouldn't write them for us."

Bruce laughed. "I doubt—"

"Bruce," Susan called down the aisle, choking on his name. "I just wanted to tell you that I thought you were wonderful."

After what she'd heard, she didn't think she could bear to hear any more of their conversation. Bruce, she now realized, was not now and probably never had been as dedicated to her script as she was. He was obviously having second thoughts about the way he would be presented to his public.

"Uh..." Bruce stammered. "Thanks."

"You haven't seen the rushes before?" Evan asked.

"Only the dailies now and then. Never put together like this," she answered.

"Well, Bruce, you should be including our writer in all the dailies. You have talent, Susan. As soon as you get back to L.A. I want to talk to you. Maybe we can set up another project."

Hearing Evan's remarks, Bruce couldn't help but believe that the negativism Evan had insinuated about the film had everything to do with his performance and nothing to do with the screenplay itself. In the face of doubt, he was trying hard to find something to keep his spirits up about his acting.

She wanted to say something more to both of them, to cry out how good her script really was and that it should be kept pure, but she couldn't. Instead she turned and hurried away.

At one-thirty that afternoon, everyone was on hand for shooting. Bruce, with makeup on, was pacing up and down the set, barking orders.

Susan didn't know how he could combine the directoring talent and the acting talent. This scene was the one in which the doctor forces Lanny to verbalize the fact that he's an addict and has lost his wife and his career. In the scene, Lanny breaks down and has to be carried away. Since Bruce had put so much effort into the other scenes, Susan wondered how he'd prepared for this one.

"Action," Bruce's assistant called, and the big lights were focused on Bruce in the doctor's office. The crew was silent, exercising caution as the cameras began to roll.

"Cut!" Bruce yelled, and the cameras were turned off. "Take five!" he called again, and Susan saw him hurry away.

For the next two hours, Susan watched as Bruce struggled with the scene. Time and again he blew line after line, never able to sink into the taxing role. She could see that he couldn't get his concentration going and as the minutes ticked away, she began to feel sorry for him. It must be a humiliating feeling, she thought.

Finally as the afternoon faded into evening, he was able to do it, but Susan knew it hadn't been his best effort. She had watched him enough over the past weeks to know he could do better.

She was aware from his expression after the shoot was completed that he knew it, also. He walked by her, his brooding eyes meeting hers for the briefest of instants.

"Don't tell me," he warned. "I already know." Self-defeat was etched in his voice.

Evan was walking behind him. "I've told him how he could fix this, my dear, but he's valiantly plugging away, isn't he?"

Susan opened her mouth to speak, but she could think of nothing to say that would help. It was obvious Dirkson, for whatever his reasons, was not giving Bruce the support he needed right now, and she could say nothing to boost Bruce in the state he was in. They walked past her.

Later, on her way back to the house, Susan had time to think. Bruce had changed drastically in the past few days, ever since he'd heard that Dirkson was coming to Santa Fe. She would be the first to admit she didn't understand everything an actor went through, particularly one of major standing like Bruce, but she did understand that he was troubled.

She'd heard so much about Hollywood stars and the fragile egos they developed over time when they were having their every whim catered to while they played the same role repeatedly on the screen. Now she thought she was seeing what happened to actors who tried to step out and take chances.

When she entered the house, Bruce was standing outside on the balcony. Not wanting another confrontation, she started down the stairs to her room.

"What's the matter? Don't want to talk about our brilliant movie?" he yelled, stopping her in her tracks. "Come on out here and we'll discuss it."

"Not tonight, thanks. I'm rather tired."

"Yeah, me too." He sauntered back into the house and down the hallway toward her. "Evan seems to like your writing, but not my acting. He says a few jokes could save me."

Anger and defeat converged inside her. "Save you but ruin the film?"

"Evan doesn't seem to think it would ruin the film." Bruce leaned against the wall, staring hard at her. He didn't know if he could trust her, but he wanted to, tried to.

"What would he know about a good film, anyway? All he's talking to you about is maintaining your star status by doing the same character over and over again. Like Donald Duck," she flared.

"And what are you doing, huh? Who do I believe in all this? You or Evan? Each one of you has your own self-serving motives."

She started toward him, then stopped. "Do you," she charged, "think I'd be telling you that you were wonderful if you weren't?"

He closed his eyes and beat his head back against the wall. "I don't know what to think right now."

"So what are you going to do? Turn this film into a slapstick comedy like I warned you of in the beginning?"

He shrugged, then straightened his shoulders and looked from right to left as if to avoid an answer. But then he said with a sigh, "I don't know what I'm going to do. Evan's invested a lot of money here."

"And you're getting cold feet?"

He glared at her. "I'm trying to be realistic."

"Is that what you call it?" she cried, hurt and angry at the way he was about to change her film and himself. "Well, I'll tell you something, Dream Lover—you can do this on your own. I have no intention of hanging around here and watching you turn my script into a farce. If you can't see that what you have so far is award-winning potential, then I can't make you."

"Susan, despite what's going on here, I need you," he declared, suddenly aware that he'd indulged himself in this moroseness of his far too much.

"For what? To feed your ego?" she exploded. "I'm going back to L.A. You do what you want with the rest of the film."

"You can't leave." He reached out for her, but she yanked her arm back.

"Oh, you mean two of us can't play the same game?" She turned and started down the stairway. "Your idea of needing someone and mine are vastly different. Too different. And this I don't need," she said with a final wave of her arm before she disappeared out of his sight.

Chapter Ten

Bruce Powers was in torment. Every night, every day after Susan left him he could think of nothing else, his body echoing with need for her. She had been, he was now convinced, the first and only woman who'd cared for him and him alone. Everything else was just so much hype.

Why he couldn't have realized it before, he didn't know. His only excuse, weak though it was, could be that he had gone through a tormented period of self-doubt, and anyone in the movie business knew that self-doubt could quickly lead to self-destruction.

When he'd come to his senses and conquered the fear of failure inside himself, he reshot several of the scenes he'd been concerned about, particularly the one

he'd done on that fateful day when Evan had arrived.
The entire time he was doing so, he told himself to
perform as though Susan were watching him, cheer-
ing him on.

As soon as he could, Bruce finished all the location
shots and moved the crew back to L.A. to finish the
rest of the interior shots. The movie was decidedly
important to him, but the foundation of his life had
shifted for a different reason, one he wanted desperately to find a way to resolve.

The moment he arrived back in L.A., he set about
trying to find Susan. In the beginning he had little
luck. She'd made sure of it. Larry Steinem told him
he'd been asked specifically by Susan not to give out
her address, and if she had a telephone it was unlisted. She was definitely unavailable.

Bruce was a man of enormous strength, but he realized his greatest flaw was in not trusting his own instincts enough. He'd gone crazy with worry over his
role in the movie, brought on by his having such an
easy time becoming a star that he'd never had to think
about any of it before, never had to work for it.

But in the process, he'd hurt Susan, a woman whom
he'd known was special from the very beginning of
their short-lived relationship. Now he set about getting his life together so that when he found her, he'd
never make any of the same mistakes again.

"Johnny," he called out the fourth day after his return from Santa Fe, "while I'm at the studio today, I
want you to do me a favor."

Johnny Day hurried into his boss's bedroom, eager to do anything. He'd been worried about his boss ever since they'd returned to L.A. There was something bothering the man, and when he was bothered, Johnny was bothered.

Flexing his thick arm muscles, Johnny stood in the doorway. "Yes, sir."

"When are you going to quit calling me sir?" Bruce complained. He was sitting on the edge of the bed, tying the shoelaces of his handmade Italian shoes.

"It's out of respect, boss."

"I know, but it makes me feel like an old man."

"No, sir—I mean, no, boss, you're not old."

Bruce gave Johnny a sly grin. "Don't try to coddle me, either. Just be yourself. That's all I ask."

Johnny beamed and flexed his arm muscles again, thinking he would do anything for the handsome man sitting before him.

"Now, I want you to do something for me."

"Sure, boss."

"Remember one time when you told me that you had friends who could find out anything, anything a guy might want to know?"

Johnny nodded.

"Today I want you to get hold of your friends and get them to find someone for me." Bruce stood up. "I want to know where Susan's living right now. I want her telephone number and her address."

"Sure, boss, okay, but why don't you just ask her when you see her at the studio?"

Bruce frowned. "Johnny, don't you think I would if I could?" His voice registered impatience. "Anyway, I want this information yesterday."

"Okay. I'll get right on it after I drive you to the studio."

"No." Bruce shook his head. "That's okay. I'll drive myself. You take care of this."

Bruce drove his Triumph to the studio, confident that Johnny would do as he'd asked. One thing about Johnny was that he always came through.

The film was going along to Bruce's satisfaction, although he was trying to do everything and more. It was important for him to get the movie out in time for consideration by the Academy, and to do that he was having to work day and night. He longed for Susan's help and support. She hadn't been in to the studio, and he couldn't find out anything about her, even though he'd tried pressuring Larry to tell him where she was.

Susan answered the telephone on the first ring. There were only two people who had access to her number. "Hello."

"Hi, it's me," Louise said. "And I was wondering if you'd agree to go to dinner tonight with an associate of ours. His name is Mark Miller—he's divine, fun, and nice to boot. He's going to have dinner with Larry and myself tonight, and I thought maybe you'd come along with us. We'd love to have you."

"Oh, Louise, that's very sweet of you, but I don't think so."

"Susan," Louise said in exasperation. "What is it with you?" She hesitated, then went on. "Ever since you got back to L.A. you've been different. I don't know what's wrong, but this behavior is not like you."

"I don't mean to be rude," Susan excused herself. "Maybe it's because I have so much on my mind. Right now I'm doing a sketch of two story treatments, trying to get them ready for Larry and—"

"And that's not all of it. I've seen you work hard before."

"Well, I'm spending the rest of the time trying to find a bungalow to rent. I don't like apartment living. I need a little outdoor space."

"Yeah, and I'm trying to help. I've got a realtor trying to find you something."

"That's great. I appreciate it," Susan said in an attempt to build up some enthusiasm.

Ever since Santa Fe, she'd been in a blue funk, listless, miserable. Devastated. That's how she was feeling. Right now when she should be thinking she had everything, inside herself she felt as if she had nothing. She was empty, drained, as if her lifeblood had been drawn from her body.

"Honey, something's wrong. I can tell." Louise felt a maternal pull toward Susan. She had felt it the moment they'd met. "Larry tells me you don't want us giving your whereabouts out to anyone." She started to add that Bruce Powers had been calling, trying to find out where Susan was, but she decided Larry had probably already told Susan about the star's calls.

Susan wanted to tell somebody how she felt. She wanted to share the pain that was hounding her. But when a woman makes a fool of herself, it's often too much to have to admit. For Susan, allowing herself to fall for a man who had women at his beck and call, and then being taken in by his charms when she should have known better... The telling of it was too much right now.

"Really, Louise, it's nothing."

"Nothing my foot, but if you don't want to discuss it, we won't. Just know that I'm here. Okay?"

"Okay. And thanks."

"Don't thank me. I haven't done anything. You won't let me." Louise gave a sharp laugh, then dropped the subject. "Now, what about tonight? I'll give you my personal guarantee that you'll like Mark. He's a wonderful fellow. Come on. Say you'll go with us."

Feeling guilty, Susan relented. "I'll go, then," she told Louise, not wanting to at all.

"Good. You won't be sorry. We'll pick you up at seven."

She was sorry already, but she had agreed to go. When she hung up the phone, she looked around the apartment she'd rented, a nondescript apartment with the customary tiny living area, tinier kitchen, bedroom and bath. She kept thinking that if she could get out of this apartment and find something to live in that maybe had a little character, she would be happier.

Right now, nothing would make her happy. She realized that. It was going to take her a long time to get over Bruce. She had no earthly idea what was going on with her screenplay. It made her sick even to begin to think about what he might be doing to it.

"Johnny, I owe you one," Bruce enthused as he patted the big man on the back. He was smiling, chuckling now and then to himself, clutching the piece of paper in his hand. "I knew you would come through for me."

"Yeah, it was no trouble." Johnny was happy to see his boss's reaction.

"How much did it cost?"

"Those boys don't work cheap, boss. A hundred dollars for the address and another hundred for the telephone number."

"Here's three hundred." Bruce peeled three bills out of his back pocket. "It would be cheap at twice the price," Bruce told him, still laughing to himself.

He'd scored a victory, a starting victory, anyway. But before he went after her, he had a few other things to clear up. This time, he vowed, when he saw Susan, there would be nothing standing between them, no other women for her to accuse him of being a playboy, no film problems and no interference from the producer. He would see to it that when he found Susan and faced her, it would be with a clean slate, one that only she could fill.

* * *

"I'm happy to meet you, too, Mark. Louise has told me such nice things about you." Susan was standing in the doorway of her apartment, staring into the friendliest eyes she thought she'd ever seen. Mark Miller reminded her of a man she'd dated a long time ago. He had pale blond hair and blue eyes that sparkled, but most important, he had a relaxed presence that made her immediately feel they'd get along well.

"Louise and Larry have told me all about you, but they didn't do you justice when they described you," he said to her.

"Thanks," she replied, feeling the way his approving eyes kept sweeping over her.

She was wearing a simple red jersey dress. After a great deal of indecision, she'd decided to put on the magnificent Indian turquoise and silver belt Bruce had given her. No matter how she felt about him, the belt was a work of art, the finest piece of art she'd ever owned, and there was no reason for her not to wear it. She'd pulled her hair back with two combs and let the curls cluster behind her ears.

"They're waiting in the car. Shall we go?" Mark gave her his arm and she slipped her hand around it, warmed by his generous smile. She could tell already that what Larry and Louise had said must be true. Mark Miller struck her as a nice man, indeed.

Larry and Louise waved to them from Larry's parked Mercedes. Mark led her across the street to them.

"Susan," a voice cried from behind.

"Yes?" She turned, and when she'd spun around halfway, her mind registered a name to accompany the commanding voice. Caught in a pivot, she stumbled.

"Susan, I've got to talk to you."

Standing on the curb, hands inside his pockets, Bruce was staring at her. His dark hair was plastered away from his face, making her think he'd driven like a madman to get there. His intense look said he was oblivious to anyone else. Only the two of them mattered.

"I..." She couldn't get a grip on her feelings quickly enough. Her heart had started to hammer inside her chest, and her legs felt rubbery. She felt Mark's hand on her elbow and she knew Larry and Louise were watching them.

She'd never imagined she'd meet him again like this. Whenever she'd visualized it, she'd thought of meeting him at the studio or at a restaurant, but not in the middle of a busy residential street. She found herself unprepared. He was just as powerful a presence as ever.

"You know it's important." When she didn't answer, he stepped off the curb, running his hands through his hair in a gesture of frustration before reaching out to her. "I've come to apologize."

"I'm busy," she finally managed, wondering how on earth he'd found her. Surely Larry hadn't betrayed her confidence.

"You can't be too busy for us." There was agony in his voice that he didn't try to hide. It made no difference to him how he looked to anyone else, whether they thought he was making a fool of himself. All that mattered was that he'd allowed his insecurity to destroy something that meant everything to him.

She looked around her, first at the perplexed expression on her date's face, then back in the direction of Larry's car. Lastly, she looked up at Bruce. "There is no us," she declared.

"Of course there is. There has to be," he said with conviction. He was waving his hands when he spoke, his face looking stormy and dark.

"Maybe you should have thought about that back in Santa Fe." It took all her strength to say what she did, and as soon as she had spoken the last word, Susan turned back to Mark. "Let's go," she told him, and he gave her a reassuring nod before leading her to Larry's car.

"I won't give up." Bruce took two steps toward them and stopped in the middle of the street. "Now that I've found you I won't give up."

He watched her get into the back seat of the car. When Larry was about to pull away from the curb, he started to run. He beat his fist against the car window.

"Susan, I'll wait for you. We'll talk."

He watched her shake her head. He saw the pain in her eyes and knew he'd put it there.

After the car had disappeared from sight, he went back to his Triumph and got inside. He'd wait, he told himself. He'd said he would wait and he would.

She didn't know it yet, probably was thinking he was a madman let loose, but he wasn't mad, just persistent. If the acting business had made him insecure with all its jaded gifts, it had also taught him persistence. It had kept him going in the past. It would keep him going now and in the future.

He leaned his head back against the leather headrest and closed his eyes. Might as well mentally rehearse his final scenes while he waited.

The night air was cooling, and he threw his jacket around his shoulders. Waiting could take a great deal of time. But it would be worth it, he said to himself. A grin settled across his face and remained there as the sun went down in the evening sky.

Chapter Eleven

The evening with Mark and the others proved a pleasant one, despite their getting off to such a poor start. Larry, always the gentleman, promised them all a good time and as expected, he delivered.

Yet, try as she might to ignore what had happened, when the car pulled away there was an image burned into Susan's memory of Bruce standing there in the middle of the street, his hand tightened into a fist, his face full of determination. She had no doubt after their confrontation that they would see each other again. Soon. But she had an obligation and since the people she was with were all gracious enough to try their best to ignore the scene they'd just witnessed, so did she.

Larry took them to a wonderful restaurant where they ate the best poached salmon Susan had ever tasted. Hours later when they were on their way to Susan's apartment, she found herself dreading going back.

Even when she hadn't been listening during the meal, Susan had done her best to keep an interested smile on her face. She had been attempting to give her companions all her attention, but the image of Bruce staring at her with that desperate expression on his face was hard to put aside.

What did he want? Why had he come back? And why now? She felt torn by a million distinct messages. All conflicting.

At her door, she said goodbye to Mark, thanking him for the evening. When she looked into his pale blue eyes she found herself realizing how much she liked him. So much so that when he asked her out for Friday night she nodded her agreement without a moment's hesitation. Maybe, she thought, maybe he was just what the doctor ordered.

Once inside her apartment, she started to turn out the lights. The telephone rang and she went to answer it, wondering who it could be since Larry and Louise were out in the car waiting for Mark. No one else had her telephone number.

"Don't hang up," Bruce said when she answered.

"How did you get this number?" Susan was beginning to wonder if there was anything he couldn't manage. In a matter of a few hours, he'd ruined what little security she'd established for herself with an unlisted telephone number and an address given to only two other people.

"What difference does it make? I have it and if you change it, I'll have the next one."

"Don't you understand? I don't want to talk to you. I don't want to see you."

"Oh, I understand, all right. I'd have to be deaf and blind not to understand that much."

"Then why don't you leave well enough alone?"

"Because I can't."

"Of course you can."

"I don't want to argue with you over the phone. I'll be there at nine tomorrow morning."

"Oh, no you won't. I won't be here."

"Where are you going?"

She was becoming convinced he was the most meddlesome man she'd come across in a very long time. "Bruce, it's none of your business." A sigh slipped from her throat when she finished talking.

"I'm making it my business." His voice became playful. "Come on, Susan, tell me."

"Oh, very well. If you must know, I'm going to be hunting for a place to live."

"What kind of place?"

"A bungalow. Maybe a small house on the estate of a larger one, anything where I can have total privacy and not be locked up inside a sterile cubicle."

"I'll help you," he offered. "I know a terrific real estate agent."

"No, thanks. I can handle it by myself."

"What time did you say?"

"I'm going at nine o'clock, Bruce."

"Maybe I'll see you tomorrow."

"No. I don't want to see you." She wanted to kick herself for spending this much time talking to him on the telephone.

"I know you don't." He paused, detecting her resistance through the phone line. "Susan, I've settled things with Evan. He'll stay out of my movie and my head from now on. I just wanted you to know that. Good night. Sweet dreams," he said before he hung up.

She listened to the disconnected hum and wondered how much more of this she was going to have to put up with. She'd have to change her phone number before she did anything else. Then when she moved, she'd make sure no one knew where she lived.

But when morning came, Susan felt like a woman on a tightrope. She kept looking out the window, wondering if she might see Bruce. She kept glancing at the phone, thinking he might try to call again. Most of all, she remembered his message about Evan. She wondered if he meant that he'd preserved the original script. She prayed to God that it was so.

At nine o'clock, a saleswoman from Centaur Realty rang the buzzer of her front door. She answered it, fighting back a twinge of regret. No matter how much she'd told herself she didn't want it to be, she'd halfway expected to see Bruce standing there. She pushed her thoughts aside as she listened to the woman describe the homes she'd be taken to see that morning.

They walked to the realtor's car.

"I always seem to be falling off the curb for you!" Bruce yelled to her from across the street.

The realtor looked as if she'd seen a ghost. She was a short woman with the usual frosted hair, wire-rim glasses and glossed lips. Now her lips were open as she stared at Bruce Powers.

"Well, that's not my fault," Susan heard herself answering. She continued toward the woman's car. On the side of the door were magnetized signs proclaiming the merits of Centaur Realty.

"I'd like to go with you." Briskly, Bruce covered the distance between them. "I have a couple of good leads for you." For the first time he looked at the realtor and nodded, then opened the passenger door for Susan. "You don't mind my going along, do you?" He looked again at the agent. This time he gave her a brief smile.

"No, no. Not at all." The woman practically fell over her own words in her eagerness to get the American Dream Lover inside her car.

Susan could see the avid look in her eyes. She knew this story would be on the woman's lips for weeks, perhaps months.

"But I do," Susan said, turning and planting her feet so that she was standing directly between Bruce and the car.

"I'm trying to help." His eyes were clear today. His mouth had a pleading quality to it. As usual, he was immaculately dressed in navy slacks and a long-sleeved navy pullover with a white collar.

"I don't want your help." She was determined to resist him.

He nodded. "I know, Susan, but don't rule out the possibility that I really can help."

"I don't want your help," she repeated insistently.

"Let me go with you. I'll ride in the back seat. I won't say anything to interfere." He tipped his head in the woman's direction. "After she's shown you everything she has to show, let me show you two places that my friend recommended for you."

He reached around her and put his hand on the door handle of the rear door. He stood there, waiting.

"No," she finally answered.

Bruce ignored her, looked at the realtor and said, "Have you a listing for the caretaker's house of Emil Whorton?"

"*The* Emil Whorton?" The woman looked as though she couldn't believe her ears.

"Yes." Bruce nodded. "He's a good friend of mine, and I called him this morning because he'd said something about leasing his caretaker's house. It's a long way from the main house, but quite comfortable. Two bedrooms and a study." Bruce glanced over at Susan. "Ideal for writing. Quiet. Quaint with high ceilings and redwood crisscrossed beams."

He opened the back door and got in. "I'll take you to see it."

Susan stood there, immobile. Was the man so skilled at manipulations that he could get anything he wanted? Out of the corner of her eye she watched the other woman as she slid into the driver's seat.

Feeling angry and resentful, Susan got inside the car. "Where do you want to go, Bruce? Why don't you give her the directions, since you've taken over this excursion."

Her words were so heavy with sarcasm that Bruce wondered if he had miscalculated this move. He'd thought it was a way to get her to loosen up a bit and talk to him. All he wanted was a chance to explain things to her. Now he wasn't sure he'd gone about it the right way at all. From the fire in her eyes and the sting in her voice, he didn't think so.

But he pushed on. "I'd be happy to. It's up in the hills."

"Oh, I know, Mr. Powers. I've driven by the estate many times," the realtor answered as she swung away from the curb.

When Susan saw the bungalow she almost forgave Bruce his brash impudence. The house sat in a stand of trees so far away from the main mansion that it could not be seen except for its roof. On one side of the house was a flourishing garden with every color imaginable in bloom. There was the smell of lilacs wafting all around them. Near the house was the swimming pool and a tennis court, which Bruce said was available for her use, as the aging actor who owned the place never used either anymore.

Inside, the house was even more lovely. There was a spacious living area, which opened on one side onto a small kitchen and dining room. On the far side of the house were the two bedrooms separated by an adjoining bath, and off the living area was the most wonderful-looking study with three walls of shelves for books and a magnificent view from a floor-to-ceiling window. It was done in cozy red chintz and dark wood furniture. Everything about the house spoke of intimacy and comfort, from the wooden beams to the stone floor and the blackened fireplace, which looked comfortably used.

"Well, wasn't this worth putting up with me?" Bruce stood behind her and to her left, a knowing smile on his face.

"The house is lovely," Susan said, trying to suppress her enthusiasm. It wouldn't do to let him see her excitement.

"Indeed it is," the realtor chimed in, clearly impressed with the house. "How much is he asking for the lease?"

"Two thousand a month, furnished."

Convinced that the realtor had nothing comparable to offer and overjoyed at the opportunity to live in this dream bungalow, Susan settled on having it. Throughout the negotiations with the owner in the main house, Susan did her best to ignore Bruce.

After their return to her apartment building she said goodbye to the realtor and started for her apartment, her mind on the ever-present man beside her, despite the fact that she should have been planning her move into her newly leased home.

"The least you could do is offer me a cup of coffee or thanks. One or the other would do."

"And if I don't?" She kept walking toward her apartment.

"Then I'll have to invite myself in." His words made Susan stop and turn. "I have some important things to say to you, and if the nights we shared meant anything at all to you, I wish you'd hear me out."

"I don't want to hear anything you have to say to me, Bruce. Just because you invited yourself along for the day and found a bungalow for me to rent, things haven't changed between us." She let her eyes take in the intensity of his look. He seemed more serious than she'd ever seen him, more troubled.

"Maybe it didn't mean anything to you, but it did to me. I've come because of us. I've taken your sarcasm and your coolness. I understand it all. But I'm not leaving until I've had my say."

The power with which he'd expressed himself rolled over her. If ever in her life she believed what a man said, she believed him now. Everything about him right down to his rigid stance said he wasn't going away.

"Then you'd better come inside and let's get this over with," she said with a stiffening of her shoulders.

"Thank you." He followed her in. Then before she could have a chance to think, he reached out for her hand and pulled her down to the sofa beside him. "I want you looking at me when I talk to you."

She couldn't keep her eyes from his. The feel of his fingers as they began to loosen against the soft flesh of her wrist and the need she saw in his eyes made her stare up at him.

"All my life I've waited for a woman like you to come to me. I couldn't define it. Didn't even try. Can't now," he said in staccato bursts that let Susan know he was nervous.

She started to sit back, but he held her still, demanding that she stay right there beside him, near enough so that he could read her reactions when he poured out his heart to her.

"Now that you've come along, you've made me see how empty my life has been without you." He shook his head. "Oh, I've gone along telling myself I was happy, living the life that others only dream about. But I never felt fulfilled. The first and only time I've felt that way was when I held you in my arms that first night." He was rubbing his fingers across her wrist, and with his other hand he reached up to brush a strand of blond hair away from her cheek. "I haven't felt that way since you left, either."

"Bruce, I think—"

"No," he interrupted. "I know what you think. I'm trying to tell you what I feel."

"Yes," she whispered, drawn in by the power of his presence. It seemed to Susan that he had a desperate need to talk, a need she couldn't interfere with.

"I got to the point where I thought I wouldn't find someone to love. I became cynical about love. It's easy to do when you live the star's life where everybody wants a piece of you, but never bothers about the real person." He tried to grin. "I'm not making excuses for myself. It probably sounds that way, but I'll take responsibility for what I've done."

Susan couldn't pull her attention away from him. It was like having someone pour his heart out into the palm of your hand, and try though she might to resist, she was glad she was there. His voice carried pain and longing, a heady combination for her.

"Your sudden leaving made me realize what I'd done. I'm glad you left me the way you did."

She was surprised.

"Because it made me think," he went on, after leaning upward so that he was better able to see her expression. Her hands felt warm to the touch, but he had no feeling for what she was thinking.

"If you hadn't left, I'd probably have gone on tormenting myself and you. I can't describe the anxieties I was feeling. No matter how long I live, I hope to God I never have those monstrous emotions inside me again. And with Evan's help, the insecurities only grew worse."

Drawn by his sincerity, touched by the timbre of his voice, Susan turned her body ever so slowly so that she was facing him as directly as he faced her. His story was touching her heart and soul with a force she'd never experienced before. She was spellbound.

"I came back to L.A. with my mind made up that I'd take care of things. When I couldn't find out where you were, I decided it was just as well, for the time being. I want you to know I've set things straight in my life before coming to you. I want nothing between us to foul things up again."

He thought of how he'd taken on Evan, accusing him of trying to subtly convince Bruce that he'd made a major mistake by playing the role as Susan had written it. "Dirkson virtually admitted he'd come to Santa Fe to see if I'd rework the film so it would be a safe and sure hit."

"He did?" Susan asked in surprise. It was the first opportunity she'd had to say anything.

"Yeah. When he's pushed into a corner, Evan is capable of telling the truth." Bruce gave her an ironic smile. "Not often."

"That's terrible. It's a cruel thing for a man like him to do."

"That's Hollywood," Bruce declared. "It's more my fault than his. If I hadn't been feeling so afraid of my own talent, he wouldn't have stood a chance." He let his hand stray to her shoulder, where it stayed. "But I swear to you, Susan, the film is exactly as we talked about. You're going to be proud of it." He decided to wait for another time to tell her about the scenes he'd reshot, trying for perfection, hoping she'd be as proud as he now was. He'd worked harder than he'd ever worked in his life.

"And there were other things I took care of, too." He thought of Linda Lansing and how furious she'd been when he'd told her they were finished and then walked out, asking her to return the key she had to his house. It was a dumb thing to have ever given her a key in the first place.

"I want you to see the film as we've put it together so far. I can guarantee there will be no surprises. You'll like it."

Susan nodded, anxious to do just that.

"I love you, Susan. I've been talking nonstop for the past fifteen minutes, hoping I'd think of a wonderful way to lead into telling you, but you're the writer. I'm just the actor." His arms went around her. "I love you."

While she listened, Susan felt a warm glow building inside her. If he'd been directing the scene, he could have done no better. His words were touching and romantic. He had eyes only for her. He was dangerously close to her. She was aware of the pungent scent of his after-shave and the movements of his chest as he talked. He was mesmerizing.

Yet she was still afraid. "So what am I supposed to do?" she asked after she'd found her voice again. "Say it's okay? That I love you, too?"

He flashed her a hasty grin. "That's precisely what you should say."

She shook her head, a picture in slow motion. "I can't."

"Because you don't love me or because you don't believe what I've been trying to explain?" He was trying to smile but it hurt. He didn't like the way she was acting—quiet, still unsure.

"Because there's no future in this thing between the two of us."

His face flared red. "Not if you won't let it be."

She hated the way she was feeling now. All confusion. Mind-boggling confusion.

"I can't let it be, Bruce. Don't you see that I'm afraid of this place, of being hurt again?"

"But with you and me it doesn't have to be that way."

"Why not?"

"Because I love you and . . ." Bruce paused.

"And what?"

"And you love me. You don't want to admit it but I can't help but believe you do, and I'm sure not saying that because I deserve you, but I think you're the kind of woman who wouldn't have gone to bed with me before if you didn't feel some sense of love for me."

She grinned, then gave him a brief nod. It was done more as a testament to his ability to read her than a declaration of her feeling.

"I told you I've been straightening out my life, putting my house in order. I think I've got my head on straight, and I promise I'll never let my actor's hang-ups come between us again."

Susan sat back and didn't resist when he followed suit, maneuvering his right arm so that it would curve around her shoulder. She sighed, overwhelmed with emotions that were weighing heavily on her mind. Her heart told her to believe in him. Her memory said she could not take rejection again, but it was clear that her heart was winning.

Bruce went on talking, not certain whether he had convinced her of anything. He loved her, and he wanted desperately to make her know it. But he could sense her continued resistance.

"The movie is going to be exactly as you wrote it. I'm working my butt off to put it together so we can have it out before Christmas."

"Before Christmas? Isn't that awfully quick? I mean why before Christmas?"

"So we can get on the ballot for this year's Academy Award slots." He smiled a teasing smile. "Slots like best actor, best screenwriter. You know."

She laughed, leaning her head back against the comfort of his arms. "That all sounds too wonderful to believe."

Susan remembered that when she had come to live in L.A., the world had seemed hers for the taking. Now she was living proof that dreams could come true. A golden glow filled her as she felt his eyes sweep over her face, a man looking for an answer.

"I love you, too, Bruce." Her face said she was as surprised as anyone at her outburst, but it was what she was thinking, and the thought was too powerful not to find expression.

"Are you speaking from the heart?" he asked immediately. "I mean, I don't want you not to be sure about how you feel. This time, let's make no mistakes."

She swallowed hard. "I'm sure," she said a bit shakily. She felt as if her heart were taking a ride on a roller coaster.

He started to laugh then, a hearty, happy laugh, looking at her with genuine affection. "I don't think you intended to tell me that right now. I think it just came out."

"I didn't have much chance to think about it, if that's what you mean."

"I'm glad you didn't." He became serious once again and brought his face nearer to hers. "I can't live without you."

"You won't have to." Now she was feeling stronger. She was doing the right thing. She loved this man. She was certain of that fact.

"Hollywood is crazy, but you and I aren't."

"I know that." Her expression was full of love.

"Come with me now," Bruce said.

"Where?"

"Just trust me and come."

She flushed with a new surge of happiness. "Of course," she said, finally free of all the doubts she'd built up, all the resentments that had at last been won over by his love.

He led her out the door and into his car. He drove fast and silently to his house. He unlocked the door, turned off the burglar alarm and led her up the stairs, still quiet but holding her tight.

At that precise moment, Susan felt all she had to do was reach out and she would hold all of Hollywood in her arms. Bruce was right in saying the two of them could do anything together, and sooner or later she imagined she might even come to the conclusion that Hollywood might not be such a vicious place, after all.

Once inside they seemed to share the same thoughts as they looked at each other with feverish eyes.

Entwined forever. Those were the words that rolled through Susan's mind when she and Bruce fell together onto his welcoming bed. There was no time for anything but their desire. They clung to each other with such urgency that Susan didn't know where his body ended and hers began.

Some clothes went, some remained, intrusive yet easily ignored in the mad scrambling of hands and arms and legs and limbs and hungry, yearning bodies. Never once were their lips apart, not even when it seemed that their voices rose in joyful unison.

Only when it was over did they take the time to undress each other, whispering playful words of love. Afterward they lay exhausted from their love quest, but content to be together.

Hands moved in gentle exploration, lips sought and were rewarded with answering passions. When time had passed and they were feeling the burning heat of desire once again, Susan rose and spread her body possessively across his. When he entered her and plunged deeper and deeper still, she felt they were united by the same consuming rapture. *Entwined forever.*

Much later, Bruce rose and left the room, returning with a snifter of brandy for them to share. They spoke of the editing work he would do the next day and of her appointment with Evan to present her new script.

Bruce asked her to hurry back to his house and his bed. He'd be home late but he wanted her to be there waiting when he returned. With teasing kisses, he made her promise she would be in his bed, undressed exactly as she was now.

* * *

Her meeting with Evan went better than she'd anticipated. He sang her praises over and over again, wanted to buy her script and promised to make it as important as the one Bruce was doing now. She left the negotiations for Larry to handle.

With a hungry heart, she hurried back to await Bruce, laughingly intending to settle into his bed as he'd asked her to do.

"Who are you?" the beautiful blonde asked when Susan entered Bruce's bedroom.

Susan gasped. She had no need to ask who the blonde was. Linda Lansing. She'd recognize the starlet anywhere.

"I said, who are you?" Linda Lansing demanded with an indignant yank of the linen sheets. She left enough of her body exposed so that Susan couldn't miss her nakedness.

"Well, you might as well come in and wait, too. He'll be back soon." The starlet adjusted the covers so that her body was more evident than before. "Bruce is quite a man, isn't he?"

Susan's answer was an angry slam of the bedroom door. Linda Lansing smiled to herself and triumphantly snuggled down into the welcoming softness of the Dream Lover's bed, the key she'd come to return safely concealed beneath her pillow.

Chapter Twelve

My God, Susan, where have you been? We've been worried about you."

"I know, Larry. I took off for a long weekend and forgot to call you. That was rude of me." She held the telephone between her shoulder and ear, trying to pack her scripts into a cardboard box and talk at the same time.

He didn't stop his scolding. "You're darn right it was. I've got a contract here from Evan Dirkson marked urgent, and I need to discuss it with you. On top of that, I worry about you. For some reason I still think of you as my naive young friend."

"All right, already," she said. There was no denying she felt guilty about not calling him because she knew it would worry him when he couldn't find her for three days. "I've been to Carmel. Prettiest place I've ever been."

"Oh, yeah? Well, if you'll hang around and write a few more scripts, honey, you can buy yourself a place in expensive Carmel or anyplace else in the world."

Her spirits rose. She tried to convince herself a smile was in order. After all, he was telling her she was a success. The success with her screenplay was no fluke.

"Can you come to my office now?" he asked.

"I'll be there in thirty minutes."

She hung up, finished stacking her scripts and papers into a cardboard box and then hauled her suitcases and the box out to her red Jaguar. The car was dusty from her trip.

She'd left Bruce's house in a state of shock. Linda Lansing had been the last thing she'd expected to see, and the worst memory was that the woman had looked and acted as if she'd always belonged there. The sight of the woman reclining so comfortably in Bruce's bed had made Susan sick, and the flagrant way she'd behaved, as if this was an everyday occurrence, had made Susan feel even worse.

She had jumped into her car and headed blindly down the coast highway, ending up in the picturesque town of Carmel, a quiet, private place to deal with her grief. But she couldn't stay away forever. She'd come back, and she knew she'd have to deal with whatever came up.

* * *

"You look terrible," Larry said when she entered his office.

"Thanks," she answered dully.

He got up from behind his modern glass-and-chrome desk to kiss her cheek. "No, I mean it. You look like hell."

Susan was aware of how observant Larry was. She could feel him taking in the lack of makeup, the dark circles that marred her face, and also, she was sure he could tell there was a deadness in her eyes. The sparkle was gone. So was her spirit.

"I know. I know. You don't have to tell me." She ran her hands through her hair, a futile effort to tame the wayward curls that had only tightened more from neglect. Self-consciously, she let her hands fall to her waist, where she straightened her blouse and tucked it tighter inside her skirt.

With a sweeping movement of his hand to signal the choice of seating, Larry returned to his place behind his desk. He punched one of the many buttons on his telephone. "No calls, please," he said into the speaker positioned to the right of the telephone.

With a flick of his fingers, he switched off the phone, cutting the two of them off from the rest of the world. "Now, Susan, tell me what's going on. Bruce Powers has called me a dozen times." Larry's voice rose. "He even threatened me the last few times I answered his calls. Always the same questions. 'Where is Susan? You've got to tell me where she is.'" Larry stopped talking, took off his thick glasses and held them tightly in his hand, looking at Susan through myopic eyes. "The man's crazy. Called me all sorts of names. Accused me of lying."

"I don't want to talk about it, Larry."

"You don't want to talk about it!" he bellowed. "Well, he certainly does."

"I don't care what Bruce wants." There was a hint of steel in her tone.

"Well, I care and the only reason I do is because something is going on here that has put me smack dab in the middle. I don't even have the pleasure of being a part of knowing what I'm in the middle of," he declared.

"Didn't you want to talk contract?"

After putting his glasses back on and adjusting them to his nose and behind his ears, he threw his hands in the air. "So you're not going to tell me what's going on?"

"I don't want to talk about it."

Susan expected her statement to anger him further. He'd been growing steadily more agitated as the conversation had progressed.

Larry knew he was close to stepping out of line—his line. He didn't like to involve himself in his clients' lives. Artists were often the worst at getting along in the world. They tended to try to make the world conform to them. A wise man would take no sides in a lovers' quarrel. From the looks of Susan's suffering he had to assume that's what this was. But he cared for her as a father would. He didn't want to see her hurt and aching, especially over a movie star whose reputation with the women was a legend.

"In case you're interested, Mark's been asking about you, too. He wants to see if he can help you move into your new place. I assume you haven't changed your plans since you called me on Wednesday. You're still moving into the bungalow, right?"

"Oh, Mark," she whispered as if she had temporarily forgotten his name.

"Okay. I'm through bugging you. Just do me a favor from now on, will you? Tell the Dream Lover that I'm not responsible for keeping up with your whereabouts."

"You won't be troubled anymore, Larry."

He swung his hands up, a gesture intended as a sign that he was putting an end to his complaining. "Fair enough. Now do you feel like talking contract?"

No, she thought. She felt like talking about Bruce, but she wouldn't do that to Larry. He had enough problems without having to give advice to the lovelorn. Advice she wouldn't take because she'd already made up her mind what she was going to do.

Susan nodded. "I'm listening."

"Evan wants to tie you to a three-project deal. You sell him this script with a promise of two more."

Although she hadn't particularly wanted to have to concentrate on business right now, she was paying close attention to what Larry was telling her. "I don't want to do that, Larry."

"You don't?" He acted surprised. "It's a terrific offer. Not many screenwriters get offers like this."

"I'm sure, but I don't want to be tied to Evan indefinitely." She was thinking of the way he'd treated Bruce. "I want to sign up for one script at a time."

"Okay, if that's what you want," Larry said hesitantly.

She was sure Larry didn't think she knew what she was doing, but it was her life and she was the one who had the choices to make about her future. "I do."

"He says he wants this script by the end of December. They'll start rehearsals around February or March."

She nodded, thinking about Bruce and how something always happened to tear them apart just when they had come together. It was destiny, she'd decided. That was the only explanation.

"Evan is going to be very disappointed and, I might add, surprised that you're not accepting his three-script proposal."

She nodded a second time, still lost in her private memories.

Larry finished explaining the contract, the changes he suggested for it and the price Dirkson was willing to pay for her script. Larry was right. If things kept going the way they were, Susan was probably going to be a rich woman. Evan was going to give her a small percentage of this film.

Larry finished telling her everything, then added, "By the way, Louise has something to tell you. She hopes you'll go by her office on your way out."

After saying goodbye, Susan headed toward Louise's office, but her secretary said she'd just missed her. Susan couldn't help but feel a sense of relief. Right now she looked terrible and felt even worse. Louise would have spotted it right off and then set about finding out what it was all about. Like Larry, Louise didn't deserve to have to listen to Susan's problems.

Susan drove from Larry's office straight to her new home. The California afternoon was fading to evening, and she had an overwhelming desire to spend the night in a place where she belonged.

The house was hidden from the street by trees. When she drove down the driveway and pulled up in front of the house, Susan's heart stood still and her head began to pound. Bruce sat in his parked car a short distance from the front door.

Slowly, she stepped out of the car, keys in hand. She'd known there would be a confrontation. She'd anticipated it, mentally rehearsing what she'd say to him. Now that the time was at hand, her practiced words were forgotten and all she could hope was that she would be able to get through this without breaking down.

It pained her to see him. He looked magnificent, like some Greek god from ancient times. A pale coral button-up cardigan over a white polo shirt, tan slacks and a face that looked like a thundercloud were all that she could see in the darkness.

She could feel his anger.

"Hello, Susan." He got out of his car and walked toward her, his steps slow but purposeful.

"Hello, Bruce," she practically sighed, dreading what was to come.

"Where have you been?" he demanded.

Tempted to tell him it was none of his business, she said, "I took a drive up the coast."

"A three-day drive?"

"I ended up in Carmel."

"Carmel's a beautiful place."

"My words exactly."

He glanced at her packed car. "Let me help you take your things inside."

"Please, Bruce. I'd rather you didn't." She put her hand out to stop him from going to her car and when she did, he took it, crushing her fingers softly against his chest.

"Susan, you've got to listen to me. Try to understand."

He'd noticed how exhausted she looked and wondered if she'd spent as many wakeful hours as he had. When he'd found Linda Lansing in his bed on his return from the studio he'd been like a wild man, going into a tirade that ended up with Linda grabbing her clothes and skulking out the door, looking back over her shoulder, thinking he would throw something after her.

Susan glared at him. "I understand, all right. I understand that you forgot something. You didn't take care of all your business when you got back from Santa Fe. There was no clean slate. You managed to leave a few things unchanged." She yanked her hand away.

"No, I didn't, Susan, and whatever else happens you're going to listen to me." In his anger, he took her into his arms, holding her so that she'd have no choice but to listen. "I did take care of Linda, or thought I did. Three days after I returned to L.A., I went to see Linda. I told her I was in love with someone. I asked her to return my house key. She said she didn't have it with her but she'd get it to me." His hands tightened their grip around her, and his words were quick and stinging. "I came home and found her in my bed. She said she'd come to return the key. After I kicked her out she laughed and said I'd had another visitor. I could guess what had happened then."

Susan was quiet, mulling over what he'd said. Something told her to believe him. Whatever his faults, Bruce had never lied to her before. Now his voice rang with conviction.

"Say something, Susan. At least say something."

"I can't handle all this," she answered. "This life..." Her voice trailed off to silence.

She was thinking back through the memories she had of Bruce, the times she'd caught a disquieting glimpse of what a future with him would be like. Their first luncheon when all eyes were on Bruce—hungry eyes, public eyes. The groupies at Tony's Bar came to mind—the insistent woman's pinched face as she'd hiked up her skirt, insolently demanding that Bruce autograph her thigh. Finally Linda Lansing, lolling naked in his bed, waiting for the star to return.

For the moment, Susan discounted the love and admiration she felt for him. Instead, confusion had claimed her. Uncertainty and sorrow were her only companions. Making a decision was impossible now. He'd explained himself, but he hadn't silenced her concern for the future.

She shrugged, fighting off tears. "It's really not the women as much as it is this place. It's not real. I'm afraid that if I stayed with you I wouldn't be able to distinguish the real from the unreal. That woman," she sputtered. "I can't get over the fact that Linda Lansing actually invited me into the bedroom with her to wait for you."

He tried his best to calm her. "But, Susan, it can be just you and me. We don't need all this."

She couldn't help herself then. She began to cry, full, salty tears that stung when they were formed and ran in hot streams down her cheeks.

"I don't know anymore, Bruce."

"You mean you don't believe me!" he said through clenched teeth.

The tears wouldn't stop. "No, I believe you."

"You said you loved me."

She gave her head a vigorous nod. "I do."

"Then for crying out loud, help me work this out," he pleaded. She was driving him out of his mind.

How could this be happening to him? He'd made some mistakes with her, but how could it end up like this? He could feel her slipping away from him before his very eyes. This was the only woman he'd ever loved and he was losing her before he really had her.

"I guess I've been hurt too much in this short-lived relationship. I actually don't think I can stand much more." She paused, then lifted her eyes to meet his. "I don't see how things could work between us. Not right now, at least. I need time."

"But, Susan, you and I together—"

She raised her hand in protest. "It seems to me we've had this conversation or one much like it before, and all you can say is that we can work it out because we're different. Well, I'm not sure of that." Feeling a new flood of tears coming on, she swallowed hard. "I can't be sure. All I know is that I don't want to keep going through things like this. This is all too foreign to me."

"What do you want, then?"

"Time."

"How much time?" he asked sadly.

"I don't know."

He released her, knowing he'd lost, wondering if he'd lost her forever. "I'm flying back to Santa Fe tomorrow morning to reshoot two scenes I think can be made better. Come back there with me."

Susan thought of the quiet, lovely times the two of them had shared there. She hesitated, knowing that her next words would be important to their future.

Finally she had to listen to the voice inside her head. "I can't," she said in a flat voice that carried no emotion.

In his frustration, he started to stalk away, going so far as to take two steps, then he stopped himself. He gave her a hard look. "You talk about reality, but this is reality—the part you're avoiding. Reality is two people loving each other enough to work things out, tough as it might be.''

She didn't answer. She didn't know what she was feeling right now, except numbness and that storm of confusion that had taken over her mind and left her feeling incapable.

"I've got to go," he said when he realized she wasn't going to respond to him.

He wanted to run back to her and take her in his arms, promising everything would be all right, but he knew Susan was too independent a woman to accept that generalization right now. She was thinking of what life would be like if she were with a Hollywood movie star, and right now she was seeing only the bad parts. There was nothing more he could do, he told himself, besides make empty promises that he couldn't guarantee could be kept.

"I'll be back in two days. I hope I'll hear from you then." He started away, then turned once again. "I love you, Susan. And if you love me, you'll call me in two days."

Bruce left, vowing to himself that he would love her for eternity, no matter what happened, even if, God forbid, he ended up without her. She was the calming influence, the sane, sure, solid woman he wanted to be his wife. She was intelligent, gifted with a bright mind, and a heart that he knew was capable of sharing a deep love.

She was his kind of woman. But was he her kind of man?

Chapter Thirteen

In Santa Fe, Bruce put all his energy, the positive and the negative, into the two scenes he was reworking. He had never been so hurt, and until the moment that he stepped before the cameras and said "Action," he hadn't known how he'd handle the agony. But once he began to act the scenes, he found his new loss added something especially creative to his acting.

For days, he worked before the cameras from early in the morning until late in the evening, and each time the lights and the cameras were turned on him he allowed the lens to focus on his pain. Each scene he worked and reworked with meticulous care, and in the end his movie crew gave him a standing ovation for his performance.

Bruce found it one of the most touching experiences he'd ever had, watching those people as they saluted him for a job well done. But he was reminded that for all this he'd paid a price—the price of a broken heart.

"Hi, Susan. I'm glad I finally caught up with you." Louise called a week and a half later.

"Yeah, well, you wouldn't believe my life the past few days," Susan told her. Standing in the center of her living room with boxes and the other remnants from her move scattered in every direction, Susan wiped perspiration from her forehead. It had taken her a lot longer to get situated in her new house than she'd anticipated, mainly because she'd been working on her script and idly staring out at the California sky, unable to think of anything other than her problems.

"Not too wild to take a few minutes to talk to a friend, I hope."

"Never." Shoving a stack of magazines off the coffee table to make room, Susan sat down. "Besides, I love to hear your voice. It always makes me feel good." Louise had a perky voice that always sounded upbeat. Right now, she would probably be the best thing for someone who was feeling as bad as Susan was, she thought.

"Good, because I have something to tell you. I'd rather tell you in person, but I'm so afraid someone else is going to tell you before I do that I'm just going to go ahead and do it by phone," Louise told her.

"I've been back home to see my mother and tell her the news."

"I can't wait to hear what it is. It must be something great from the way you sound."

"I think so. Larry and I are getting married. We decided the weekend before last."

"Oh, Louise," Susan cried. "That's wonderful. I'm so happy for you."

"Thank you, darling. I knew you would be."

"No two people are a better match than you and Larry," she said, believing it.

"Well, we shall see." Louise chuckled. "You're right, I think. Larry and I do have such a good time together. He's a wonderful man."

"Yeah. When is the big day?"

"The day before Thanksgiving. You'll have to promise to be a witness for us. We'll have just a small group, but you'll be one of the most important ones there," Louise enthused.

"I'd like nothing better." To Susan, Thanksgiving seemed a long way away. Each day she'd been counting the days since she'd seen Bruce. Nine days and a few hours. She hadn't called him when he'd returned from Santa Fe, and she hadn't heard from him. He was, she was certain, waiting to hear from her.

Susan hung up the telephone and went back to her unpacking. In two hours she was finished, emptying the last box and putting everything in its place. She went to the kitchen, brought out a bunch of orange tiger lilies she'd bought at a corner florist and then got out a bottle of champagne and a solitary glass she'd bought for the occasion.

Ceremoniously she put the flowers into a vase along with some water and put the champagne and glass on a silver tray, then she took them with her as she went back into the living room and sat down.

The house had grown more comfortable with each box she'd unpacked. Now thrown across the leather recliner was an afghan her mother had made for her, and on the coffee table were the latest books she'd been reading. Upstairs on the oak table next to her bed, she'd put pictures of her father and mother and a single one of her younger sister. If she'd loved the bungalow before, she loved it even more now that it had her touches added to it.

The time spent settling into the house had been a period of sadness for her. Susan had never experienced the kind of torment she'd suffered for the past week and a half. She had tried once, then two more times to contact Bruce, but his phone had been busy and she'd stopped herself from trying again.

She still couldn't see how they could work things out between them. She knew she loved him. She felt he loved her, but she couldn't visualize a future that wouldn't include doubt and fear. Falling in love with a famous Hollywood star was not like falling in love with the man down the street. There would be enormous differences and adjustments that would never end.

Wiping back a tear that came from nowhere, she opened her champagne, watched the cork hit the ceiling and fall to the floor and poured herself a glass. "Happy house, Susan," she said to herself as she fought off the hollow feeling inside her and wiped away another tear.

Over the next few days she threw herself into her work, anxious to get on with her life. She heard from Mark once. He asked if he could come over and she told him yes. He'd be the first to see her house.

The next afternoon, just as he'd said, at half-past five, Mark was standing at her door. That warm friendly smile of his was like badly needed fresh air.

"May I come in?" he asked softly.

She welcomed him in, needing the companionship that someone like him could give, and for the next two months Mark proved himself to be her most stalwart friend.

He was there whenever she needed him, never asking for anything from her except that she allow him to be her friend. He was her escort for movies and plays. He showed her a different side of L.A. than she'd expected, a nice side.

What he couldn't do was make her happy. No one could except Bruce, and he was out of her life. She hadn't laid eyes on him since the night he'd come to her house and they'd argued so vehemently.

"Mark, I have a crazy favor to ask of you," she said one night after they'd been in a movie and were sitting out on her back patio.

"You know I'd be happy to do anything for you." He smiled at her, and the smile reminded Susan of her father.

"I want you to find out what you can about *Temptress*."

"Like what?"

"I'd like to know where Bruce is with it, what the scuttlebutt is about it. Anything, everything."

He gave her a knowing look. "I'll check into it first thing in the morning."

"Thanks," she said, hating the fact that she couldn't let things die between herself and Bruce, yet afraid, still terribly afraid.

After so long a time had passed with no word from Susan, Bruce told himself he must face up to the facts. Late one night after a particularly trying day of editing *Temptress*, he had gone home, refused the dinner the cook had ready for him, and instead had fixed himself a double Scotch on the rocks. He took off his shirt and went into his exercise room, where he got inside his rowing machine, and stopping only to finish off his Scotch, he rowed until he didn't think he could move another muscle.

Exhausted, he stretched out across the machine, taking pleasure in the discomfort he found when his backbone touched metal.

Distraught, with more worries over getting the film out than any man should have to bear, Bruce had been over and over the facts of his relationship with Susan. His feelings had run the gamut from grief to fury.

At one time, he'd even considered the possibility that Susan didn't love him but had only been fooling herself that she wanted the Dream Lover. But Bruce had more common sense than that. He believed her when she'd said she loved him. He also believed, as he lay in an uncomfortable heap across the rowing machine, that he'd never find another woman to love the way he loved her.

Yet what could he do, he asked himself again and again. She was an intelligent woman who knew the consequences of a life with a movie star. Would he make her hate him if he were to try to convince her that she would be happy with him?

He sighed. Here he was working around the clock, trying to finish this film, trying not to listen to the Hollywood gossips predict he'd filmed a loser, and he needed her by his side. What he didn't need was this agony.

Bruce wasn't sure what he was going to do, but it would be in the best interests of both of them. He loved her that much and more.

It was several weeks before Mark came to her with the information Susan wanted. Every time she'd seen him since that night, he'd told her he was working on it, but so far he had only rumors to go on.

"Okay, I've found out what you want to know," he told her over drinks one evening.

"I'm about to die of curiosity."

"Because it took me so long?"

She nodded. "I didn't intend you to have to spend much time with this. I just wanted a general idea."

"Like I said, Susan, I know this is important to you. I wanted to make sure I was reporting what was really happening."

"Which is?"

"*Temptress* has been filmed exactly as your original script was written. There were no changes."

She sighed with relief. Bruce had told the truth. He'd been able to conquer his insecurities. It made her feel good for both of them.

"He's been working twenty-hour days to get the film editing done. The publicity will hit nationwide next Friday."

"Next Friday," she repeated. A premonition swept over her. She'd be seeing Bruce soon.

"There's going to be a sneak film at the Westwood Theater on Monday night."

"A sneak preview?"

"Yeah. Where the audience comes in and watches the film, then fills out cards giving it a rating. Hollywood insiders claim it's a good predictor of a film's success or failure."

"What else have you heard?" she asked, trying to keep the excitement she was feeling from overriding her thoughts.

Mark stared at her, then shrugged before speaking. "I heard it's one of the best films to come out of this town in a long time. I was told that by someone I trust, Susan. She said that Hollywood is going to be rocked on its heels."

Tears threatened and Susan stood up, struggling with her emotions. Could it be? Could it all be working out as she'd dreamed?

"I'm going to the screening."

"I'm sure you'll be notified, Susan. Evan will let you know."

The next morning proved Mark right. A messenger delivered a note telling her about the screening and also told her of a premiere scheduled in Santa Fe for December 5. Attached to the note was a plane ticket and a reservation notice for the La Fonda Hotel. Evan wanted her to be at the premiere. She wondered if that was a good sign or a bad one or any sign at all.

Susan's apprehension couldn't be allowed to show in public, and over the next weeks she was caught up in parties and fetes for Larry and Louise's upcoming marriage. She asked Mark to go with her to the sneak preview of *Temptress*. It was scheduled only two days before Larry and Louise would tie the knot.

When Monday came, Susan felt nervous as a cat. She could do nothing—work, rest, play—nothing. As she dressed for the screening, she could hardly button her blouse, and try as she might, she couldn't get herself under control.

They went in late, when the house lights were going down. Susan saw Bruce and a few of the others who'd worked on the film over in a far corner in the back of the theater. Evan was nowhere to be seen, and she averted her eyes whenever she thought Bruce might be observing her. She wanted to see the film, not the filmmaker, tonight.

Within seconds after she sat down, she became oblivious to everything around her. There was no Mark, no Bruce, no theater, only *Temptress*. From the moment the credits were flashed on the screen and the haunting music began, she was captivated by the vision of her story being brought to life.

Soon she was engrossed with the masterful performance by the man she loved. If ever there was any doubt, he was proving his talents, immense talents. Over and over again he brought her to tears as the heart-wrenching beauty of the film flashed across the screen.

Afterward, she let Mark lead her out the back way so that she wouldn't be seen. With emotions brought to the surface for anyone to see, Susan didn't want to be around anyone. How could she explain a woman who was ecstatically happy and brokenhearted at the same time? She couldn't explain it herself.

Temptress was a winner. She was confident of that fact. Everything about the final product said so, and the audience had enthusiastically agreed. But seeing her idea brought to life proved to be both exhilarating and sad. Each scene brought back memories of better times.

The next weeks blurred by as Susan helped Louise prepare for her wedding to Larry. When the long-anticipated day arrived in typical California style—all sunshine and bright blue skies, Susan was as nervous as a bride-to-be herself.

Mark, who was proving himself to be the best kind of friend, was Susan's escort for the small, informal wedding. The ceremony and reception took place in Larry's sumptuous back yard, filled with what must have been hundreds of clay pots with fresh white flowers. The entire wedding party numbered less than forty, the intimate gathering being, in Larry's words, a way for his close personal friends to be a part of the most important time in his life.

Dressed in a handmade dress of fine old ecru lace, the beautiful bride laughed and danced with her new husband, and every time Susan glanced their way she felt a trace of envy that quickly turned to guilt. She couldn't help but long to have happiness rule her life the way it did Louise and Larry's.

"Be happy," Louise told her just before she left with Larry to take a European honeymoon. "You need to find happiness. You can find it through love. I know I did."

"But, Louise, what if a situation stands in the way?"

Louise had studied her for a long time, then taken her into her arms and hugged her fiercely. "Susan," she'd whispered, "if you love Bruce, really love him, then no situation can stand in your way."

Susan watched her friends hurry to their waiting limousine, and all she could think of was what Louise had said. Louise, the one who'd said nothing about Bruce, hadn't mentioned his name in months, Louise knew it all.

Had she guessed it, Susan wondered. Or was Susan the kind of woman who wore her feelings on her sleeve?

With a final wave, Larry winked at her, and Louise threw her bouquet straight at Susan. With no difficulty she caught it, just as Louise had so obviously intended her to.

Susan bent her head to sniff the fragrant bouquet, absorbed in the thought that it might be too late for her to get Bruce back. It had, after all, been a long time, a very long time.

"If you love him," Louise had said. God knows, Susan told herself, she knew she loved Bruce. Could that be enough? She closed her eyes and smelled the bouquet once again, oblivious to the noise of the remaining wedding guests standing around her.

Love. She loved him. That was the only certainty for her right now. The only one.

Chapter Fourteen

L.A. at Christmastime for Susan was like anticipating ice cream and finding it to be sherbet instead. The weather was warm and sunny, but the only red and green appeared on fire hydrants and jade necklaces.

Instead, the "in" colors for celebrating were hot pink, chartreuse and an overabundance of silver and gold. The hotels kept a few pink poinsettias around their heated pools but let nothing interfere with their basic California style.

So it was with added eagerness that Susan looked forward to attending the Santa Fe premiere. When she boarded the airplane, she looked around for someone she knew, but there was no one. And when she stepped into the La Fonda Hotel in Santa Fe, her eyes scanned the lobby for a familiar face, but there was none. She ignored her disappointment, loving the red and green decorations gaily festooning the hotel. Red and green meant Christmas was near.

Dressing that night for the premiere, Susan kept taking deep breaths, telling herself that she and Bruce would probably ignore each other. There would be nothing for her to worry about. Yet worry she did. Seeing him again and talking to him had been in her mind for two weeks. Now that she'd admitted to herself that she wasn't going to get over him, she could think of little else.

She put on a sequined gown Louise had talked her into buying for the occasion. Done in a midnight-blue fabric with silver sequins arranged in an abstract pattern from shoulder to hem, the gown fitted Susan like a glove. Even Susan, who normally paid little attention to her clothes, felt that she looked like a million dollars.

Evan called from his hotel room and told her the limousines would be outside to pick them up at eight o'clock. At eight she was ready, having pulled her hair back with two rhinestone combs that complimented the gown.

Outside the hotel stood Bruce. "I was about to come upstairs after you," he said by way of a greeting. "Evan's gone on ahead. You and I are to go in this car together."

There were flashbulbs popping everywhere around them. The glare was so bad that Susan was blinded as she groped her way into the back seat. But Bruce must have sensed her difficulty, and taking her arm, he saw that she was safely seated.

As soon as he was inside, he turned to her, ignoring the still-active cameramen and the autograph seekers who clustered around their car. "Hello, Susan. It's good to see you."

The gentle way he spoke—his eyes traveling across her face as if to make sure she was the same woman—was enough to make Susan's throat thicken with unshed tears. She fought them back.

"Hello," she managed.

"You look beautiful."

"Thanks," she said without looking at him. The chauffeur slowly drove the limo through the crowd of people.

"Of course, you know if I had my way you wouldn't have all that makeup on. I like the natural you."

She smiled then, drawn in by his winning ways. "I know."

He reached over and took her hand. "Wish us good luck tonight."

She smiled again. "I do, Bruce." It was as if they'd never been apart. With him beside her, everything seemed at peace, even her hurting heart. She was surprised how calm she was feeling.

"I've seen you on television," he told her.

"I've seen you, too." After the sneak preview, the street talk was that *Temptress* was a runaway hit, and Susan had found herself plunged into interviews and talk shows almost daily.

"From the looks of things, you take to the celebrity life very well," he said as he released her hand.

His voice had carried with it a trace of irony. She wondered if he had thought the same things she had. Since the first days of telephone calls and interview sessions, she'd made a comparison of her life to Bruce's. Not that it was on anything like such a grand scale of public attention as his, but she was getting a taste for it.

"I'm glad you think so," she said, laughing. "The first two times those people turned the television cameras on me, I didn't know what I was doing. I still can't remember anything I said."

Now it was Bruce's turn to laugh. "I know the feeling well."

The rest of the trip was made in silence. Bruce was lost in his thoughts. He'd imagined he could handle this situation without too much difficulty. Susan had made her choice. Now he'd have to find a way to live with it.

Seeing her had made him rush to take her hand, a foolish but instinctive response. Seeing her made him know that without her his life would never take on any of the greatness he'd dreamed of, even if *Temptress* did for him what he'd prayed it would do.

Susan was thinking that she might not be able to handle the rest of the night being around him. It seemed so good, so intimate, the way they'd come together, but the intimacy was a cruel reminder of how empty her life was without him.

As they stepped out of the limousine, Bruce turned to her, his face solemn as he spoke. "After tonight, Susan, you're going to have your own share of unrequested adoration. I'm going to be anxious to see how you deal with it."

He gave her no time for response, but expertly led her through the crowd of fans, stopping once before a television camera and introducing her to the reporter as the hottest screenwriter of the future. She warmed to his compliment, and murmured her hellos to the camera before he led her on into the theater.

Inside, there were many introductions and handshakes as they made their way through the press, the critics, the distinguished citizens of Santa Fe, Evan, a handful of his followers and an even dozen of the people from assistant directors to gofers who'd worked on the film.

Finally the light dimmed and the movie began. Susan sat holding her hands tightly webbed together. She heard Bruce cracking his knuckles, and from where she was seated she could see Evan squirming in his seat. They were all nervous. They all had everything to gain, and everything to lose.

At the movie's end there was a moment's silence and then the people stood. To a round of thunderous applause, Bruce and Evan followed suit. Before she knew what was happening Susan was being propelled from her seat to stand beside Bruce as she felt his arm slip around her.

Afterward there seemed to be an army of reporters around the three of them, and Susan stood in stunned silence while she heard Bruce sing her praises to all who would listen. He told how she had come to Hollywood with the best script of the year and how she'd stood beside him helping to make *Temptress* the hit everyone was predicting it would be.

She was filled with such joy that she didn't know if she could speak, but when the cameras and the microphones were switched to her, she in turn was able to tell how brilliantly Bruce had performed his roles as both actor and director.

It seemed the night would never end because each reporter who seemed satisfied and ready to leave was pushed aside by three more who wanted one special message for their viewers or their readers. Finally they were whisked away by studio executives and led back to the hotel. There were too many people around Bruce and Susan, making talking impossible.

She didn't see him again before she left for Los Angeles the next morning. Over the next few weeks Susan was plunged into instant celebrity status. Everywhere she went she was hailed and greeted by well-wishers and people who'd now heard of the new screenwriter. Suddenly her name was on everyone's lips.

Christmas was spent with Larry and Louise. She tried not to let them see what she was feeling. They expected her to be happy with her newfound success.

That evening when she returned to her bungalow, she was met by a harried messenger who said he'd been trying to find her since early in the morning. The messenger had a package for her, and as she signed for it, she was sure she could guess who it was from.

Her heartbeat throbbed in her ears as she stood there with shaking hands opening the package. Inside a black velvet box was a large diamond solitaire necklace mounted in platinum. Tucked into the top of the box was a folded note.

Her hands still shaking, she took the note out and opened it.

"Susan," it read. "We should have been together today. The Academy Award nominations are made in January and announced on February 6. Since you won't call me, I'll call you one more time. By February I think you will have had a big dose of celebrity status, and hopefully you'll see that while it's difficult, it's still manageable. No matter what, I love you. Bruce."

She went back inside her bungalow, clutching the note and the velvet box against her chest. Oh, God, she thought, let there be a way.

Until midnight, she sat beside her Christmas tree with the lights from the tree the only illumination in the house. It was her first Christmas without family, and though she'd enjoyed Larry and Louise's company she still felt a pang of homesickness. She'd called home, but it wasn't the same.

Christmas should be spent with people you love, she told herself. Immediately the image of Bruce settled into her mind.

* * *

On the day the ballots were sent out to members of the Academy, Susan received another knock at her door and answered it, only to be greeted by a messenger with a letter. Inside was another note from Bruce.

It simply said, "Order your gown."

This time she smiled. He was telling her she was going to be nominated for an award.

Others must have thought so, too, because she was suddenly overwhelmed with requests for photo sessions, magazine and television interviews, one on top of the other. The studio publicist for *Temptress* called and asked if she would be willing to fly to New York to appear on *Good Morning America* and the *Today* show on the same day. When she tried to decline, she was told the shows would interview her at her home.

Within the next month, it seemed Bruce's prediction had indeed come true. She'd had a myriad of experiences, from having newspeople digging through her trashcans to chasing away photographers who had stationed themselves outside the windows of her house.

On February 6, Susan sat by the telephone, waiting for Bruce's call. Shortly after two o'clock it came.

"Susan, it's Bruce."

The sound of his voice richocheted through her. She closed her eyes. "Hello, Bruce."

"Susan, I have good news." There was excitement in his voice. "You've been nominated for best writer."

"I have?" she asked incredulously.

"I told you you would."

"I know, but I couldn't let myself believe it." She was stunned.

"And *Temptress* was nominated for best picture," he went on.

She hadn't recovered from her surprise, but already she was praying that he would tell her he, too, had been nominated. "Oh, Bruce, that's wonderful."

"I've been nominated, too," he said, and Susan thought she could hear a certain tightness in his voice.

"Tell me," she whispered, still praying for him.

"For best actor—"

"Bruce, Bruce, I told you!" she cried.

"And best director."

"I can't believe it." By now she was sputtering. "This is the most wonderful news I've ever heard."

"I knew you'd be happy."

"And you?" she answered.

"Yes, I'm very happy." He was wanting to ask her if she still loved him, but he couldn't make his mouth form the words. He was too afraid of the answer.

"I can't believe this. It's too unbelievable," she said, still dazed by the news.

"I knew it. After you left me in Santa Fe, I finally came to my senses and realized it." He paused, then went on, "Have you ordered your dress?"

"Not yet." She began to laugh. "But now I certainly will."

"I want you to go to the Academy Awards with me."

She felt an immediate rush of disappointment. She'd thought from his note that he might want to see her. She was hoping she'd have the chance to tell him that she'd changed her mind. Now she was able to visualize them together. He'd been right all along. As long as they loved each other— "That would make me very happy," she said.

"Between now and then we'll both be busy."

"Yes, I'm sure we will."

"Maybe on the way to the ceremony we can talk about what you think about being a celebrity. If you weren't one before, you're certain to be one now."

"Things couldn't get much worse."

"I'll be willing to bet they can."

She wanted to keep him talking, holding him to the phone. She wanted him. Surely he must have guessed it by now. "Bruce, I've never had the proper chance to thank you for the necklace."

"I got your note."

"It's beautiful. Too much."

"I hope you'll wear it the night of the Awards. Goodbye, Susan."

He hung up the telephone, having ended one of the most difficult conversations of his life. He'd wanted to blurt out how much he loved her, tell her how he longed to have her with him, but he hadn't. They'd been separated this long, and he wanted to give her time to experience firsthand what it was like to have the attention drawn to her without wanting it. If he stood any hope at all of getting her back, it would only be after she'd been through the experiences that were coming to her right now. Maybe then she'd see.

When he saw her again he planned to ask her to marry him, and if she said no, Bruce wasn't sure what he would do.

By the time the Awards night came, Susan had had more flashbulbs go off in her face than she ever wanted to see again. She'd been pushed and shoved by jostling photographers until she was black and blue. She'd been misquoted and had had a host of clandestine love affairs, according to two national tabloids. Things had finally gotten to the point that she was becoming a little immune to all the attention.

One thing was certain. She knew what the celebrity life was like. Suddenly she could do no wrong and everyone was asking her to write a script for them— any kind of script.

Compared to the turmoil she was going through over Bruce, though, the celebrity status seemed a minor nuisance. She looked on him with new respect each time she lived through a particularly embarrassing experience. Now she was intent on telling him so when she saw him again. She wanted nothing more than to end this separation, to find peace with him at last, if he'd have her.

She would be willing, she told herself a hundred times, to make a trade-off with fate. She'd give up the chance for an award if she could only have him. Nothing would ever be as important as having him love her.

* * *

Johnny Day steered Bruce's heavy Rolls-Royce into Susan's drive. "Do you want me to get her, boss?"

"No," Bruce said as he hurried out of the car. He licked his lips and brushed his hands through his hair. His nerves were like needles piercing his skin. Taking a moment to straighten the stiff collar of his gray tuxedo, Bruce rang her doorbell.

"Hi," she said when she came to the door. Bruce stared at her. She wore some makeup, but not much. Instead she'd kept the natural look he loved so much. Her beautiful toast-colored hair she'd left, too. It danced and curled around her face in a way that pleased him. She looked as beautiful and innocent as the first day he'd laid eyes on her. Her gown was of palest blue satin with a simple band of rhinestones to outline the neckline and the cuffs of her sleeves.

"You look beautiful," he said.

She smiled. "Thank you." She made no movement then. He was looking at her and it seemed they were both spellbound. She resisted the urge to throw herself into his arms. That was all she wanted from this night.

He cleared his throat. "Shall we go?"

She reached up and touched her fingers to the diamond necklace he'd given her. "Yes," she said, and slipped out the door ahead of him.

As soon as they were inside the car, they both began to speak at once.

"I've got something to—"

"I wanted to go to the—"

They laughed. "You go first," she told him, feeling the steel edges of fear and panic about to engulf her.

"No, you."

"Please," she said.

"I wanted to go to the Academy Awards with you by my side."

She took a deep breath. "Me too."

"I've been doing my damndest to stay away from you, to give you enough time to—"

"I've had more than enough time," she answered quickly, letting her hand reach out for his.

"You have?"

"Yes." She looked at him, allowing the love she felt for him to shine in her eyes.

They pulled up to the curb and a sea of photographers gathered around the car. Bruce was oblivious to them. Susan looked around nervously.

Johnny opened the car door and Bruce got out, then turned to give her his hand. "I love you, Susan."

"I love you, too," she cried, but her voice was drowned out by the buzzing crowd.

They sat toward the front of the audience, eyes only for each other. Bruce took her hand in his and held it tightly.

The announcement for best screenplay came first and when Susan heard her name being called, she couldn't make her legs move. Bruce stood and helped her up, then he drew her into his arms and brushed his lips against her cheek. "I knew it," he whispered, and motioned her toward the stage.

She stood at the podium looking around at the audience, knowing she was standing before millions of people. She said a brief thank-you, unable to say anything of consequence. Then she stood still a moment longer, looking out at what surely must be the epitome of Hollywood itself. Silently she paid it homage. Hollywood might have set her back a little temporarily, but it hadn't defeated her. Susan McCarthy had made it. With a quiet smile, she carried her Oscar close to her heart and walked off the stage.

Bruce couldn't contain his excitement. He kept touching her, rubbing her arms, holding her hand. He was like a man crazed with happiness. "I'm so proud of you, Susan. You did it," he kept saying over and over again, and she loved how pleased he was for her.

When the announcement came for best actor, it was her turn to hold his hand as he became subdued and still. Only Susan could know how much this Oscar would mean to him if he were to win. It would be a solid way of his seeing that his belief in himself had paid off.

When the announcement was made and Bruce Powers's name rang out through the theater, Susan watched as it dawned on Bruce that it had actually been his name. The cameras panned to him, but he sat motionless, a slow smile, that secretive smile of his, etching its way across his face.

Then to a roaring crowd, Bruce stood, blinked once and strode to the podium. He received his Oscar and began to speak, his emotions visible on his face.

"I want to thank the Academy for this award," he said in a choked voice, "but most of all I want to thank the woman who gave me Lanny, then gave me the strength to play him. Susan," he said, and all eyes turned to her, "come up here beside me."

She hesitated, but only briefly. The look in his eyes was enough to convince her that he wanted to share this moment with her. She hurried up and heard the thundering applause as he took her into his arms and kissed her.

He turned back to the audience. "Without Susan McCarthy there would have been no award for me." The two of them walked off the stage, their Oscars in one hand, their arms solidly around each other.

Susan felt it was the most meaningful experience she'd ever had, and she was tempted again and again to cry. But there was too much joy between them.

Temptress's winning best picture was just an enormous added pleasure as she stood backstage with Bruce beside her, answering questions being tossed at them from a hungry press.

With hundreds of people clamoring for their attention, Bruce turned to her. "Can't you see, Susan, that if we love each other enough we can be together no matter what kind of crazy, glitzy world we live in? I love only you," he cried over the interruption of press and people. "If you love me, you'll know that we owe it to each other to work this thing out."

She tightened her arm around his back and smiled up at him. "I love you, Bruce. I want nothing more than to be with you."

Before hundreds of flashing lights he bent and kissed her, the touch of his lips sweeter than anything she'd ever experienced. Tears filled her eyes then.

"How are we going to work this out?" she asked, pointing to the crowd that was milling around them, intent on their every word.

"Day by day. Minute by minute. We'll be fine."

"What'll we do about the groupies?"

The people who could hear bits and pieces of their conversation had grown quiet, eavesdropping as intently as they possibly could.

"We'll let them baby-sit when we go to the movies." He held her close.

"What about Hollywood?" she asked, deciding that if they were going to settle this thing it might as well be here and now. It would save the press the job of snooping around later. "You told me once that when you could leave on top, you'd quit."

"What about you?"

"I'm just beginning."

"Me too. I want to get best director next year. You can help me do it." He gave her that famous secretive grin of his. "Now kiss me and say you'll marry me."

Susan put her arms up to embrace the Dream Lover, and for the first time since she'd come to Hollywood, decided that she'd follow his orders. They sounded too good to resist.

Silhouette Brings You:

Silhouette Christmas Stories

Four delightful, romantic stories celebrating the holiday season, written by four of your favorite Silhouette authors.

Nora Roberts—*Home for Christmas*
Debbie Macomber—*Let It Snow*
Tracy Sinclair—*Under the Mistletoe*
Maura Seger—*Starbright*

Each of these great authors has combined the wonder of falling in love with the magic of Christmas to bring you four unforgettable stories to touch your heart.

Indulge yourself during the holiday season...or give this book to a special friend for a heartwarming Christmas gift.

Available November 1986

Silhouette Desire

Available
October 1986

California
Copper

The second in an exciting new
Desire Trilogy by Joan Hohl.

If you fell in love with Thackery—the
laconic charmer of *Texas Gold*—you're
sure to feel the same about his twin
brother, Zackery.

In *California Copper*, Zackery meets the
beautiful Aubrey Mason on the windswept
Pacific coast. Tormented by memories,
Aubrey has only to trust . . . to embrace
Zack's flame . . . and he can ignite the fire in
her heart.

The trilogy continues when you
meet Kit Aimsley, the twins' half
sister, in *Nevada Silver*. Look for
Nevada Silver—coming soon from
Silhouette Books.

DT-B-1